A TEN CENT MIRACLE

Roslyn Nelson

ISBN:1981971602
ISBN-13:9781981971602

Published by F. Richard Allen
Walnut Creek, CA
rallen617@gmail.com

DEDICATION

To my daughter, Laura Nelson Alpert and my son-in-law Dan Alpert and equally to my daughter, Susan Shanfield and her husband Stanley Shanfield for their love, help and support.

ACKNOWLEDGMENTS

I would like to thank Richard Allen, without whose help in organizing and typing and retyping, this book would never have been born. I also want to thank Mary Webb, the teacher and the members of our writing group and the Published Writers of Rossmoor, for their encouragement and support.

CONTENTS

A TEN CENT MIRACLE

In the mid 1930's, when the depression was at it's height, my family lived in a cold water flat behind my father's tailor store, in a crumbling eight-family tenement building, in an equally crumbling section of Brooklyn.

Toward the store and the flat I had conflicting feelings. On the one hand they represented the only security I knew, however shaky. On the other, they were a confirmation of our abysmal poverty. It seemed to me, we would never be able to climb out of it.

Once out the kitchen door, however, there was no conflict, only love. For out of that junkyard, that neighborhood dumping ground, where the fruit man emptied his rotting produce beside the rusting frames of ancient bicycles, out of the weeds and stones and broken glass, came a ten cent miracle.

In the antiquated red brick of P.S. 70, the miracle began with the most prosaic announcement. School children would be permitted to purchase seeds for a penny a packet, exactly a tenth of the regular retail price. While a dollar would have been a prohibitive

sum for me, one that would have taken me all summer to save, ten cents for a whole garden could be
managed within a reasonable length of time. It would
take care and forethought, of course, but it could be
done. And, ten candy-less days later, I was in posses-
sion of a silver dime.

No queen ever carried her crown with greater
joy than that which I felt as I bore my precious seeds
home. My long-suffering, good-natured mother, bone
weary from her long day in a sweat-shop, shrugged
and told me in her old country parlance that I could
"verdreisach dine kopf" (bother my own head), about
them. At least it would keep me busy for one or two
afternoons.

A spade and snow shovel were our family's
whole complement of garden tools. Holding them
and my seed packets, I set out on my great adventure
with nature, a plump and serious little girl, determined to make a thing of beauty in the midst of an
iron and concrete world. A glance, however, was
enough to remind me that my seeds and tools would
be of little value for quite a while.

The plot was 40 X 100 feet, a jungle of debris and
weeds that would seem to admit no master. A garden

was an impossibility. I should have put the seeds away and forgotten the whole thing, but I was only nine, and I dearly wanted that garden. I set out to get some empty bushel baskets from the fruit man for the rubbish and I announced my purpose to anyone who would listen.

Soon the baskets were full. Pushing and tugging, I discovered that I could not get them curbside by myself. At first, no one offered to help, but finally, partly out of sympathy, partly out of a desire not to be annoyed again, my mother lent a hand, and the first two bushels were out on the street for the trash collectors. Two more afternoons of silent toil went by and four more loads were gone.

Mr. Werthheimer, first floor left, the quiet little father of eleven children, offered to help me "clear up a little more." An early casualty of the depression, he had been out of work for as long as I could remember. He sat staring out of that backyard window hour after hour. It was strange to see him actively working, friendly and talkative. At his suggestion, trash barrels were pressed into service. We began to see a dent in the junk in the yard.

Through several late afternoons, Evie's husband, Eddie, lame and handicapped, the only adult male in the neighborhood we addressed by his first name, had watched from the first floor right window. Now he "figured that I might as well help for a little while". Four of the nine Werner kids, top floor right, who were frequently in minor trouble with the police, discovered that collecting trash could be fun. It became a contest to see who could fill the barrels fastest.

Two whole weeks ticked by, and inch by inch, the miracle grew a little larger. Not a tin can or a piece of scrap remained. We looked around us with a growing sense of triumph, and it was then that we really became aware of the cast iron weed.

We didn't know its botanical name. Tough and rubbery, with a thick, sappy stem, a curious mixture of red and green, it grew six to eight feet tall in a matter of weeks in Brooklyn, out of concrete and under railway overpasses, and on city lots, where nothing else would grow. It had always been in the yard, and we took it for granted, like the ever-present junk, but we had never before had reason to test the tremendous vitality of its life force.

With great confidence, we set out to dig it up by the roots. We dug deep in the hardpan soil with our shovels, but no end to the roots appeared. Very well, we would chop off the stems and expose the roots we could find, and the weed would die. But the plants resisted cutting with the toughness of steel. From the exposed roots new little leave appeared.

Discouraged, but determined, we pulled at the weed with brute force. They proved a formidable enemy.

The Werner kids had long since departed. Mr. Wertheimer paused in the midst of hacking at the weed and said in his kindest voice, "It's too far gone to be a garden, but at least it will make a nice play yard."

Yes, I thought, that's true, but I have the seeds already. Maybe if I just chop the heads off the weeds whenever they appear and ignore the roots, I can still have a garden.

Mr. Wertheimer went back to his window. Eddie helped me turn over the soil around the edges a shallow foot or two. "You know," he said, with the wonder of a city man, "all that garbage musta been good for the dirt. It looks pretty rich and black."

The next few days I worked alone, planting all of my seeds. An occasional neighbor glanced from the window, and, I suppose, felt sorry for me, because they knew that nothing would grow in the yard except the weed. As the days passed and no other sign of life appeared I grew irritable and restless. My mother took my temperature and predicted dire diseases, but except for my outbursts of temper, I was perfectly well.

Then, one day, where Eddie and I had made the flower beds, a hint of green whispered above the surface. Two delicate little leaves arched, humpbacked, out of the ground. I was thrilled beyond telling, fulfilled beyond hope.

Soon, row upon row, the little seedlings pushed their way out of the ground. The yard was the first place I went in the morning, the last place I visited at night. At lunch time I always found a few minutes for it, and after school, I thinned and weeded and staked for hours. I was a little crazy on the subject, obsessed, as all lovers are.

Though the yard belonged equally to all the tenants, Mr. Wertheimer asked me, deferentially, if I would mind if he took a patch for tomatoes. Then

Eddie planted a packet of corn. Old Mr. Myers, who had the only real garden for blocks around, gave me cuttings of a few perennials.

The ground proved fertile indeed. Before July began, the garden had started to bloom. Marigolds lifted their heads like tiny golden suns against the summer sky. Morning glories draped purple crinolines across the old tar wall of the garage. Lavender cosmos and red zinnias, white sweet alyssum and blue corn flowers carpeted the once-barren soil. Mr. Myer's lady slippers and never-dies grew lush and lovely, too.

Suddenly, everyone in the building had a hobby. Skinny Miss Kelly, who lived with her aged mother, brought shells from the beach to make a neat edging around the center circle of zinnias. Mr. Fassiole, who was a bricklayer, burly and hard-drinking, brought bricks from the job to make paths. The weed was an every-lurking menace, but everyone in the building kept it hacked down.

When the dog days of summer came, I trotted back and forth from the kitchen sink with a watering can, dripping water and tracking mud on the worn linoleum floor, so full of joy that I didn't notice the heat. As the corn and tomatoes matured, they were quietly shared as "surplus" with those families in the building who were barely subsisting on potatoes and beans. Old Mrs. Klein, who was dying of cancer, lived out her last summer in the garden, and Eddie's baby played among the flowers.

At summer's end, we collected the seeds in carefully marked envelopes, and the next year we planted them again. For the three more years I lived in the building, the ten cent miracle continued to thrill the neighborhood.

Sometimes I think of the garden, now. The neighborhood has probably gentrified and the garden is no long there, but for me, the memory of it and it's message of hope and beauty and possibilities will always remain.

THE PRESSING MACHINE

As I sorted through my mother's few possessions, I came upon a tattered photograph, dog-earned
and brown with age. I had never seen it before, but I
knew, instantly, when and why it had been taken.
Tears welled up in my eyes.

The photograph shows my father, a small, dapper, balding man, with a trim mustache, standing
proud and unsmiling, in front of an old-fashioned
pressing machine. In one of those stiff poses of the
period, he wears a dark pin-striped suit and starched
white shirt and behind hm can be seen the shabby tailor store, in back of which we lived.

It was 1935, in the depths of the Depression.
Our pressing machine represented the difference to us
between rent and eviction. Nothing else about the
store brought in enough to matter. An old machine, it
looked like two ironing boards, the upper one standing at a forty-five degree angle to the lower. They
were mounted on a scarred wooden counter which
rested on a metal pedestal. At the base of the pedestal
were two foot controls which brought the top board

down over the bottom one and then up again: that was how the pressing was done.

Standing at its side was the life force of the machine, a round, rusted boiler., which created the heat and steam. It was ancient. It wheezed and creaked asthmatically when it worked at all. More often, it gave up the ghost altogether and awaited the ministrations of the repair man. At best, it took hours for the boiler to heat up, which meant that my father could not compete for while-you-wait business.

Methodically, my father added numbers on the backs of old envelopes, trying to find a way to pay for a new machine. In installments, of course. There was no doubt that it paid to do so. It was strictly a matter of finding the money.

Two years passed, and the problem was no nearer solution, until one day, the old machine settled the whole matter for him. There was an ominous cracking sound from the boiler, and the old machine was through. No amount of coaxing by the repair man would bring it back: it was finished, dead.

The grim lines around my father' s mouth grew deeper. In vivid phrases, my immigrant Russian-Jewish mother cursed Columbus, the store, and the machine. Like a line of army ants, numbers crawled up and down the envelopes until three in the morning as my father sought a solution. Finally with an intense sigh, he said what I had known all along he would say, "A loan. There is no other way."

The loan, from a finance company, was nothing new, for we often borrowed from one to pay another. But this new indebtedness, for eight hundred dollars at six percent interest, seemed to us like madness. We were already deeply in debt, our income lagging far behind our expenses. After much discussion, and with great misgiving, my grandmother co-signed for the loan.

Soon the machine arrived. It was not beautiful, but it was shiny and new, and remarkably efficient. In any case, we stood in awe of anything that commanded such a price. Though I must have been in school at the time, I'm sure that it was about then that the picture was taken.

It was obvious, soon enough, that the new machine earned its cost, and yet, each month, when the loan payment fell due, an air of gloom settled over the house for days. The figures climbed the envelopes, but in the end, it was always the same. Somehow, some temporary solution was found - a loan from a relative, an unexpected tailoring order for my father, some overtime work for my mother and the problem was resolved again until the next month. For two and a half years, the loan and the possible loss of the machine loomed over our heads.

One month, however, a great day came. After the usual period of gloom and reprieve, my father made a momentous announcement: "Next month, we make the last payment on the loan."

With hope in my heart, I began to look forward to the end of the month, forward to the payment of a bill. At last the machine would begin to work for us, instead of for the loan company, a good machine that would not need repairs. For the first time in my childhood I began to see a way out of our poverty.

About two weeks before the end of the month, on a lovely fall Sunday, my sister and I spent the afternoon playing with a friend. At about five o'clock, the bell rang. A neighbor boy stood at the door, red-faced, puffing, out of breath.

"Your mother wants you right away," he panted. "Something happened."

We pleaded with him, "Tell us what!" But he only said, "You mother said not to tell you. She wants you to come home right away."

Hearts exploding, we ran all the way home. My mother stood at the door, seemingly impassive. Bluntly she told us, "Dad collapsed from a heart attack. He's in the hospital now, and I have to go there. The doctor says he's very sick, and can never work again."

It was two years later that my father died, but before the first month of his illness was over, our lives had turned upside down. We gave up the store, for no one would buy it, and moved to an apartment near my grandmother's house, several miles away. My mother sold the store fixtures, including the pressing machine, for whatever they would bring.

When the buyers had gone, my mother stood for a moment at the threshold of the store. She sighed once, deeply, and then locked the door firmly, without looking back.

With the proceeds from the sale, some two hundred dollars in all, she paid the movers, the first month's rent on the new apartment and the last installment on the loan.

A SUMMER DAY'S ODYSSEY

The summer that I was six, the asphalt paving in the street gutters melted. People slept out on their fire escapes to get some relief from their airless humid rooms. There was no air conditioning in those days, but even if there had been, in that poor section of Brooklyn during the Great Depression, no one could have afforded it. The only way to escape the blast furnace of heat was to go to the beach on Sundays.

During the week, no matter how hot it was, people had to work, but on Sundays, from all over Brooklyn, people headed for Coney Island. No one had a car. Our magic coach was the subway.

We'd load a paper bag with sandwiches, tote our blanket and a beach chair for my mother and take the trolley that ran in front of our house to the elevated as it headed out to the beach.

The train was always full, and I could feel the sticky sweat on my forehead, and smell the stale odor of perspiration all around me. Bodies jostled bodies, as the train jerked to a stop at each station. When we arrived at the last stop, a faint whiff of salt air drifted

up to us on the platform and we followed the hurry-
ing crowd as they crossed under the elevated.

We had to traverse a vast expanse of burning
sand if we wanted to be anywhere near the water. We
stepped over blankets and bodies that had already
staked out a piece of real estate, searching for a place
to spread our own blanket. As far as the eye could
see blanket bordered blanket. From the air it would
have looked like one enormous crazy quilt.

The sand toasted the soles of my feet as I raced
toward the water, but the Atlantic was deliciously
cold. I'm fair-skinned and sunburn easily so my
mother had insisted that I wear a white tee shirt over
my swimsuit, even in the water. I jumped the waves,
happy to be cool, joining the hundreds of others who
couldn't swim and remained fairly close to shore. I
stayed in the water until I was blue and shivering.
Back at our blanket, my mother toweled me off and
handed me a sandwich. For the first time all week I
felt cool enough to eat and did so hungrily.

All afternoon I returned repeatedly to the crash-
ing breakers. When it was time to leave, my mother
held a towel around me, so that I could wriggle out of
my wet suit and into my street clothing. We couldn't

afford a locker, and the towel was supposed to provide some privacy.

We struggled up the still scorching sand and entered the elevated. Like-minded families, dragging children, blankets, pails and shovels, crowded in around us. We were packed into that train like jelly beans in the jar of a guessing game contest. Our sunburned bodies radiated heat. I could feel the sand rubbing against my skin.

At the second stop my mother took my hand and led me out to the platform so we could catch a breath of fresh air. As the doors of the train began to close, I let go of her hand and darted inside. The doors snapped shut. My mother was still on the platform, frantically clawing at the doors, but they wouldn't open. The train started. In the midst of that mob, I was all alone. My six year old mind panicked. I thought I'd never see my mother again.

Through an open window my mother shouted, "Get off the train at the next stop and wait for me."

With that, the train roared away from the platform. In spite of my sunburn I was trembling. At the next stop I got off, but so did a man who had been standing near me.

"What's your name, little girl?" he asked.

I didn't answer because I'd been taught not to talk to strangers.

The man made no move to leave the platform. My mother had told me about kidnappers. Was this man one? If the train didn't come would he take me away with him? Why was he waiting here? I had no idea if or when the next train would arrive.

After what seem like eons, I hear a familiar screech and rumbling as a train approached. My joy turned to bewilderment and my heart sank as the train slowed at the station but didn't stop. The man came closer. He leaned toward me. I was frozen with fear.

"It didn't stop because it was an express," he said. "Your mother will be on the next train."

I didn't know whether to believe him. I didn't know what an express was. Time seemed to stand still. After an endless wait, the local finally arrived, and there, miraculously, was my mother. I think she was as frightened as I was. She scooped me up in her arms and burst into tears. I had never seen her cry before.

The man approached my mother.

"I waited on the platform because I was afraid she'd leave and go to look for you," he said. "I have a little girl about the same age."

My mother thanked him, and seizing my hand, led me back into the train. All the tears I had been holding back spilled over. Nothing my mother said could comfort me.

When we finally arrived home I was exhausted. That night the bedroom was stifling. I ran a fever and my back was completely blistered but it didn't matter. I was home again. I was safe.

CAROLINA

"Carolina," I scolded, "that's not like you. You can't make generalizations like that. I'm Jewish. You're African-American. How do you feel when people generalize about you?"

"Well," she looked at me squarely, "but they do, don't they? And besides, you don't live with them in Santa Ana like I do." Her voice was indignant. "Them Mexicans! Every house's got run-down old trucks and rusty car parts in front. Nobody ever cuts the grass. There's weeds all over. Nobody ever plants a bush or a flower."

I knew she was exaggerating. Carolina was given to grand effects. Still, I understood why she was so angry. She'd often told me about her house. She was so proud of it.

"The mortgage is almost paid off," she'd say. "When it is, I'm going to retire. My husband has a good job at the train depot. Been there for thirty years. Without the mortgage payments, we can make it easy.

"I made the house so pretty. Not grand like yours, you know," she'd say, looking around at my ordinary suburban tract house, "but I planted grass out front and lots of flowers. It's real, real nice. Prettiest house in the neighborhood."

Then she'd scowl. "But some people, they just trash up their place. It makes me mad. And now the pushers are comin' around, and you have to be nice to them. Two of them were sellin' right out on my front lawn. I told them my grandchildren was comin' and would they please move down the block. I mean, I was real polite, 'cause they got guns and they know to use them. I hear shots in my neighborhood all the time."

Carolina had worked for me for ten years, every Wednesday, dependable as the earth's rotation. She was never late, and if she had to cancel, which was rare, she'd call me early in the morning, and set up a replacement date.

She probably carried three hundred pounds on her five foot, six inch frame, but she was as fast and agile as a hummingbird. She climbed stepladders with ease to polish a chandelier, or wipe the top of a ceiling fan. I didn't have to direct her. Carolina would see what needed doing and do it, willingly and cheerfully.

Sometimes she would tell me she was a little short of breath. "Sort of wheezy, " she'd say, and I thought maybe it was because of all that weight, but she thought she had an allergy.

For years we had a little ritual. When she'd come in, around nine in the morning, we'd sit down and have coffee and a bagel together, or maybe a muffin, and we'd chat for fifteen minutes or so.

Long ago she'd told me she was part African-American, (Black was the word she used), and part Cherokee. Her skin was a lovely sort of blush-brown, unwrinkled, even when she finally left me at sixty-three.

She'd grown up in Oklahoma, she said, and she remembered her Cherokee grandmother, and how the old woman had revered the earth. Carolina thought maybe that was why she loved flowers so much.

In spite of her name, Carolina had no trace of a southern accent. "Oklahoma don't talk that way," she'd sniff disdainfully when she heard a Southerner on the portable radio she carried around while she cleaned. "I ain't had but a sixth-grade education, but I don't drag my voice like that."

She was intuitive, observant and quick-witted. I used to think that if she'd had more education, had not been African-American, she might have gone far in the world.

One day, during our morning coffee, several months before she left for good, Carolina seemed uncharacteristically quiet and sad.

"What's wrong?" I asked. "Are you feeling OK?"

"It's my husband. I think he's doing drugs. Sixty-five years old and never touched stuff like that, and now he's doing it."

"How do you know, Carolina? Or do you only suspect?"

"Don't have no proof. But Darrell's been regular as clockwork on the job. He missed two days last week and three this week. Sat around the house, half asleep all day.

"Maybe he was sick, Carolina."

"You live in my neighborhood, you get to know what a junkie looks like. Besides, I gave him money for the mortgage payment last month and I just got a late notice. Where's the money gone to? No, he's doing it, all right, only I don't know how long it's been going on."

A few weeks later when she came, she said, "Come on outside and look at my car."

I knew she drove a beat-up old Cadillac, but I couldn't imagine why she wanted me to see it.

"Look," she said, pointing to a line of even-ly-spaced perforations in the driver's side door, "machine gun holes. I think Darrell owes the pushers and this is a warning. Don't matter much about the car. It's about ready to fall apart anyways and I ain't got the money to fix it."

Sure enough, a few weeks later, Carolina started coming by bus.

Several months went by and then, one day, Carolina said abruptly, "Darrell lost his job.

Couple of years from his pension, and he's out of the job."

I didn't understand. "Were they trying to get rid of him so they wouldn't have to pay his pension?"

"No." I'd never seen her so down. "It was his own fault. He's hardly gone to work in months. I told you. He's on drugs. He took out a second mortgage on the house to get money to pay the first one. But he spent most of it on the crack. Now he's talkin' about a third mortgage, and we was almost paid off on the first, before all this started."

I didn't know what to say. She was such a hard worker. It didn't seem fair that it was happening to her. "Is he working at all, Carolina?" I asked.

"Well, he's got hisself a broken-down old truck, and he goes around collectin' junk: old refrigerators, sinks, toilets, things like that. Dumps 'em out on the lawn till he gets enough to go to the scrapyard and get some money for them. Killed the grass. Killed my flowers too…"

For a moment I thought she was going to cry. Then she sort of shook her head. "Well, got to get to work." She started to rise.

"Wait, " I touched her arm. "Why don't you leave him, Carolina? He's only dragging you down."

"Can't."

I could hardly hear her.

"Don't have enough money to rent a apartment by myself. I was plannin' to take a place with this friend of mine. She left her husband, and we was goin' to move in together. Only thing is, she went back to him, so..." She stared off into space. "Don't know what I'll do. All my flowers..."

She'd been wheezing more than usual that day, and she seemed very tired and lethargic. I thought maybe it was psychological. She certainly had cause. But the next Wednesday she didn't come and she didn't call. I was worried about her. I knew something had to be drastically wrong.

When I called her home, the voice that answered was deep and had a strong drawl. "Carolina's in the hospital." The voice seemed detached and spacey.

"What's wrong with her?" Now I was really alarmed.

"Doctor say she have some kind of heart thing. Con-something heart trouble."

"Congestive heart failure?" I suggested. That would account for the wheezing.

"Yeah, that it I think. Anyways, he say she can't do no housework no more, so I guess she won't be comin' 'round to you." He sighed. "Don't know when we gonna do for money, though, seein' as how we both cain't work no mo'."

It was a pretty broad hint, but I didn't bite. I knew if he got his hands on any money it wasn't Carolina or the house that would get it.

"What hospital?" I thought I'd speak to her directly and offer her some help.

He said, "You cain't call her there. She ain't got no phone."

"Well, can I visit her?"

"No you cain't. Ain't possible." And with that he hung up the phone.

Several weeks went by and then one day the phone rang and it was Carolina. "I'm sorry about leavin' so sudden," she said. "Doctor says I can't work no more. Couldn't even call to let you know. See, I didn't have no insurance, so I went into the hospital under my sister-in-law's name. The one that's been livin' here with me. You remember. I told you she was getting disability from the government. So I used her card. Didn't nobody know my real name."

Her situation appalled me. "Carolina, " I said, "I'd like to help. I can't send a lot, but…"

"No." Her voice was hoarse and raspy. "He'd only get his hands on it and use it for the drugs. Don't send anything."

I called a few times afterward, but each time that man's voice answered and said she wasn't home. Then, the last time I called, the voice said, "You don't need to call no more. Carolina's dead."

I was shocked. Was he telling the truth? I didn't know, and I didn't know how to find out. Maybe it was true, because I never heard from her again, and it saddened me to think that that was how her last days had ended.

Every now and then, especially on Wednesdays, when my present cleaning woman comes, I think of Carolina, and I remember a day shortly after she told me her husband had started to work collecting junk. Rain had been coming down in great squalls all day and I didn't want her to have to wait in that downpour for the bus, so I offered to drive her home. "You're tired and it's pouring out there. Let me take you."

Carolina resisted forcefully and at first I couldn't understand why. Then it dawned on me. The outside of her house now fit the description of the trashed up houses she had condemned for so long, and she didn't want me to see it. Her pride wouldn't allow it.

She deserved better out of life. Her industry and dignity should have been rewarded. But life isn't a fairytale, and no one ever brought a glass slipper to change the life of a brown-skinned Cinderella.

THE LAST TRAIN

Hannahlisa sits in front of her vanity table, trying to repair her makeup. She's been weeping for hours, and her eyes, those famous gentian blue eyes, are red and swollen.

She'll wear a hat when she leaves, she decides, one with a large brim, and sunglasses to cover her eyes. She'll let her blonde hair show through, though. Odd, she thinks, how she, a Jew, looks infinitely more like the Nazi's "Aryan" ideal than Hitler, certainly, and more even than Kurt, whose hair is a sort of dirty blond, and whose eyes are brown.

She hadn't thought about her Jewishness before the Nazis. Her father is a world renowned scientist, her mother a writer, Hannahlisa, herself, an actress. They had traveled in intellectual circles and were non-observant Jews, free thinkers really.

Hannahlisa had considered herself German, rather than Jewish. When her parents left Germany the year before, they had begged her to come with them. "It's dangerous to stay," they'd said. But she'd refused adamantly. She didn't want to leave Kurt, and she knew he would protect her. She was sure of it.

At the thought of Kurt, she has to control the tears again. She is thirty-six now, and has been Kurt's mistress for how long? Ten years? No, eleven. He'd been a minor functionary in the Nazi Party then; the Party itself not yet really important.

They'd had such wonderful times back then. He'd taken her to all the Party social functions. Often she'd been the center of attention, the focus of an admiring crowd.

But then, as Kurt rose in the Nazi hierarchy, as the Party itself gained power, and its philosophy hardened toward Jews, he had gradually stopped seeing her in public. First it had been Party socials, then cabarets, then restaurants. Finally he would come only to her apartment, always out of uniform, in a dark suit.

"I love you," he'd told her. "I don't agree with the Party's policy toward Jews. It's just some of the fanatics. But I do subscribe to the rest. And I've given so many years of my life to it. I can't leave now."

So he'd continued to visit her, and to bring her gifts, though they were not conspicuous ones like the flowers he used to bring, but small, hard to find luxuries, easily concealable under his suit jacket, such as silk stockings. He'd brought her two pairs on his last visit the day before, along with a train ticket.

Hannahlisa examined her face in the mirror again. She had been a great beauty. Was her age showing now, she wondered? Was that why Kurt had told her that she must leave on the train at fourteen hours? "Get there about ten minutes ahead," he'd said. "Don't come earlier, or linger on the platform."

"But I don't want to leave you. Why must I go?" she demanded. And what about my furniture, my paintings, my books. Who'll look after them?"

"You must go, Lisle, you must," he said, using his pet name for her. "Some of these fanatics in the Party... Lisle, I'm risking everything to tell you this. The train at fourteen hours will be the last one out of Berlin, before the Party begins checking identifications, and removing Jews from the trains."

He was in a position to know such things, she knew, but was he telling the truth, she wondered, or had he found a younger mistress? Was that why he wanted her to leave? Was he deceiving her, as he'd deceived his stodgy wife all these years? Or was this simply a ruse to get rid of her because she'd become a liability?

Stodgy. It was his word. And cold, he'd said. A frigid woman, with a distaste for sex. Her house, her possessions were her all-consuming passions.

Now, did he tell some younger woman the same story about her? Or did he simply not mention her at all, only talk about his frigid wife?

Still, Hannahlisa knew she couldn't afford to take a chance. Already she'd seen Jews mistreated and humiliated in the streets. Better to be on the train. She could always come back if he'd lied.

She dressed carefully, as always: a sky-blue suit, a matching hat with a large brim, the silk stockings Kurt had given her, and high-heeled shoes. She'd packed a bag the night before, putting in several changes of clothing. It was time to go.

Putting on her sunglasses, she picked up her suitcase, and headed down the stairs. On the third rung from the bottom, a wayward strip of metal sticking up from the carpet runner caught her hose, and ripped a large run in them.

Because of the timing, she hesitated, but she had always been fastidious. Turning back to her apartment, she removed the stocking, and replaced it with one from her suitcase. She would have to rush, or she'd miss the train.

On the street, she hailed a cab. "To the train station", she said, "and hurry. There's an extra ten marks if you make it by ten before fourteen hours."

Traffic was heavy, and though the driver changed lanes frequently, they couldn't make much speed. To save time, she paid the driver before they reached the station, giving him an extra twenty marks. Jumping out of the taxi, she was relieved to see that the gate which held back tardy would-be riders was still open.

In her high-heeled shoes, she ran to catch the train, but just before she reached the gate, it swung shut, and a moment later, the train, the last train for Jews to escape, went roaring out of the station.

BUTTERFLY

"When Katie yells for Evelyn," my mother used to say, "It's so loud the Japanese beetles fall off the the rose bushes."

Katie was our next door neighbor, a vivacious brunette in her early thirties, buxom, with delicate features. Her cheeks were so rosy she needed no rouge. She had mischievous black eyes, with deep laughter creases at the corners, and thick, curly hair, whose dark strands constantly escaped the kerchief she wore at all times.

Katie laughed often and when she did, her voice boomed out over the neighborhood like Gabriel's trumpet. Evelyn was her nine year old daughter.

Even as a small child, I wondered why Katie had married her husband. He must have been in his seventies, a tall broomstick of a man, unkempt, taciturn and humorless. My mother used to send me to his grocery store for milk, which in those days, in the thirties, came in tall, silver-colored cans. The old man scooped the milk out with a metal ladle, and poured it into the pitchers his customers brought to the store.

What fascinated and nauseated me, was that Kleinman, that's what everybody called him, no Mr. or first name, had a misshapen index finger on his right hand with a black and diseased-looking finger-nail on it. He would shift his inevitable cigar stump to his left hand, while he unhooked the ladle from it's place on the wall. They he'd put the stump in his mouth, with it's half inch of ash overhanging the milk pail, and ladle out the milk with his right hand, with that awful looking fingernail. I was sure the ash would fall into the milk, and the blackened nail made me feel sick.

Like us, the Kleinman's lived behind their store. Sometimes, when I was in our backyard I could hear Katie singing in her kitchen. She was different from the other mothers, a butterfly among moths, high-spirited and fun to be around. Every now and then, when we girls were playing jump rope, she'd join in the game for a minute, and when we played the game known as potsy in Brooklyn and hopscotch in other parts of the country, she'd take a turn at that, too.

Then, one day, both Katie and Evelyn were gone. When they hadn't returned by the end of the second day, curiosity got the better of my mother. She grabbed the milk pitcher and with me in tow, headed for Kleinman's store.

"Where's Katie today?" she asked, as Kleinman ladled out the milk. She struggled to keep her tone casual.

"Gone." came the laconic reply.

"Gone where?" My mother couldn't stop herself.

"To her family." He hung the ladle back on the wall.

"When is she coming back?" It was not a time when people traveled readily. Money was scare in those depression days.

"Not." His cigar ash hung precariously as he capped the milk can.

"Not what?" My mother was stunned

"Not coming back. Took her bastard and walked out on me, after I took them in when she didn't know where to go." It was the longest speech I had ever heard him make.

"Bastard?" My mother's eyes widened. Her mouth formed a letter "O".

Kleinman handed my mother the pitcher. "You didn't think Evelyn was mine, did you?"

"I... I took it for granted." My mother stammered. "Why would I think anything else?... Kleinman..." My mother hesitated, but tact was not her strong suit, and I could see that she was bursting with curiosity. "I don't mean to pry or hurt you, but why did Katie leave you? She seemed so happy."

Kleinman shrugged and flicked the cigar ash onto the floor with that crooked, ugly finger. Some of the ash dusted his shirt. "Women," he said, "who understands them?"

THE PACKAGE

Let me just say this in my own defense: the package did arrive at a most inopportune moment.

My wife, Karen, was already groaning in labor. I had her blue overnight bag in one hand and was pulling the door open with the other, when the postman almost tumbled into the house. He was off balance, you see, because he had been leaning toward the door.

He gave me a funny look and said, "Package for you. Big 'un." Then he noticed Karen's swollen belly and smirked, "I'll say."

Annoyed, I scrawled my name on the form he shoved in my face, glanced at the brown-paper parcel only long enough to see it was from Boyd and slapped it on top of the bookcase. I pushed the postman out, held the door open for Karen and we hurried to the car.

But let me back up a minute. I want to be honest about this. The truth is—-this is hard for me to admit—but it was because the package was from Boyd that I was annoyed. I wanted to be disentangled from him and his gifts and his strange moods.

I hadn't seen Boyd for almost a year and I certainly wasn't expecting anything from him. He'd been one of my graduate students down at Lee College in South Carolina, a Fellow in the Writing Program. I was the Faculty Advisor. After some initial skirmishing—at first he seemed ill at ease with Northerners, or perhaps it was just city people, we'd struck up a relationship of sorts.

One day, when we'd been discussing a problem he was having with a story he was writing, he suddenly said, "Come on, let's go hunting."

I'm a city man, not from the West Virginia "hollers" like Boyd and I didn't know or care much about hunting, but I went along as a way of getting to know him better. I thought that in that informal setting I might be able to penetrate his shell. I found this harder to do then I anticipated.

He was a lanky man with a full blond beard and intelligent gray eyes that somehow managed to be challenging and self-deprecating at the same time. He talked a great deal in the car going up to the mountains without revealing anything about himself. He seemed to want my friendship, but when I asked him about his background, he fended me off by adopting a nasal twang in place of his usual drawl and said, "Wal, they's Mammy and Pappy and mah girlfriend, Daisy May." Then he changed the subject.

When we reached the spot he'd picked, I could see the defensive layers peeling away from him. He was silent for the most part, but it was a serene silence. At one point he said to me, "I feel at home here. It's the only place I feel at peace."

I think that was why he'd taken me there, for though he was a crack shot—he'd brought down a duck with each of the two shots he fired—it was clear that he hadn't come up for the hunting.

I liked Boyd, in many ways admired him, but I felt that I didn't really understand him.

After we'd known each other for perhaps three months, he laid a small gift-wrapped package on my desk. In answer to my raised eyebrows, he said, "It's a geode with an amethyst inside. I found it one day when I was hunting. Nature is full of mysteries, isn't it? I've collected rocks from time to time. There's something elemental about them."

He flipped his hand to the side in a deprecating gesture. "Never mind the bullshit. Would you be interested in seeing my collection?"

I went to the little one-room caretaker's cottage he was living in—he was housesitting an estate to save paying rent—and he began to pull out a collection of rocks.

"That one's calcite," he said, handing me a rounded rock that had been split in two whose center made me think of ice-capped mountains. "And this one's black obsidian. I found it down in the holler."

To the dim light filtering through the shuttered window, he held up a crystalline form I would have taken to be onyx or jet.

Then, abruptly, he turned his back to me. "I want to show you something else."

He stepped to a sort of cupboard or armoire with ornate mahogany doors and brass handles which seemed out of place in that modest cottage, revealing, as he opened it, a collection of rifles, maybe eight in all with barrels of varying lengths and thickness and stocks of different colored woods.

He watched me closely as I gingerly handled one of the guns, feigning an interest in it, although it actually repelled me, but I could tell from the sudden sag of his shoulders that I hadn't deceived him. He snatched the gun away from me and as suddenly as he'd opened them, closed the mahogany doors. I sensed that some kind of door had closed over those intelligent eyes as well. I had the feeling that I had taken some kind of test and failed.

Once we went out drinking together. He belted the whiskey, three shots of it, as though he wanted to be part of the low class crowd in the bar. He became loud and belligerent, but though his speech was slurred, his grammar, in that Southern drawl, remained impeccable. Soon he grew melancholy and silent. As abruptly as when he had shown me the guns he said, "Let's get the hell out of here!"

Somehow I wasn't prepared for the exquisite spare stories that he began to show me. They were stories about the hollers and their people, full of keen observations: the glint of an osprey's feather as it descended; the way the sunlight slanted off the mountains; the trick of speech that told someone was hurting. In particular I remember a character in one of his stories, a boy of eighteen, who sits at a bar, feeling totally isolated, wondering why he can't find pleasure in the shared hunt, or the beer bashes or the bowling, like the other men. I guessed that it was autobiographical, but he didn't seem any more at home among the college intellectuals.

Soon after that I had to go to New York on business. I decided to detour into West Virginia to see, at first hand, the countryside about which he had been writing. Like most people, I guess, my knowledge was limited to the stories about the McCoys and the Hatfields, the blood feuds among the illiterate mountain people and the poverty, of course. Vaguely I thought about child brides and whiskey stills. I knew all of the cliches. But I had not expected the exquisite and solitary beauty of the landscape: the steep-sided hills clothed in azaleas and rhododendron; the pristine blue mountains capped with dark and brooding evergreens. I hadn't envisioned the lonely distances and minimal roads that separated neighbors, or the poverty so intense that nothing was thrown away. Looking down from the hills at the little houses cradled in the hollows, I could see that the yards were strewn with castoffs: broken refrigerators, worn out tires, rusted auto shells that might, some day, prove useful. I thought I was beginning to understand Boyd's feelings of isolation.

Back in New York, I showed some of Boyd's stories to a friend who was editor of <u>People and Places Magazine</u>. I wasn't surprised when he said, "Tell your young man to get in touch with me. I'd like to publish some of them."

Four of the stories appeared in the magazine over the next year and a half and Boyd was beginning to build a modest reputation. After the third story was published, he presented me with an antique cigarette lighter shaped like a pistol. I didn't understand why he had given it to me, since he knew I didn't smoke. There was a note with it that said:

"To Jim,

With thanks for patience and friendship."

The sentiment surprised me.

After the fourth story made its appearance, he slid a flat package across my desk, then left without a word. Inside were three photographs, blown up and framed, of birds in flight: hawks, I thought, wheeling and dipping over the mountains. I had the notion that somehow the birds were connected with Boyd himself. I was sure he had taken the photographs. This time the note said:

"Hang these up if they appeal to you."

So, I did, right there in my college office.

Later that same day, Boyd called to ask if I liked them.

"Very much so," I told him. "They're already up on my office wall."

"Office," he said in a flat tone. Again I had that strange feeling that I had somehow failed him.

My time at the college was drawing to a close and I didn't seek tenure. Boyd and I had talked about our mutual distaste for the clannishness at the college, the polarization of blacks and whites, Southern gentry and "Crackers".

"I don't fit in with any of them." His voice rose sharply. "Not with the spoiled rich playboys who are here getting a little polish with Daddy's money. Not with these black intellectuals with the chip on their shoulders and not with the "Crackers," either. Always got their noses to the grindstone, when they don't forget and start swilling beer. All they want is to turn into one of those rich boys. All they want is a piece of the pie. No, I don't fit in with any of them."

I was surprised by his vehemence. I hadn't guessed that the reasons for our distaste were so disparate.

I saw Boyd a few more times and then left for my new position as an Assistant Professor at a Boston university. I was happy to be going back up north.

I didn't hear from Boyd again until nine months later, when that package arrived in the mail.

Karen delivered a boy in the early afternoon—it was the twenty-second of April, and later that day I headed for the college, sailing along in a sea of euphoria, delighted to be a father, happy that my wife had come through so well and the baby was healthy. I was pleased with my ability to support my family while working at a job that I loved. In all the excitement, the package lay forgotten.

About three weeks later I received a phone call from a former colleague at Lee college.

"I thought you'd want to know," he said, "since Boyd was a protege of yours. He killed himself this morning."

There was a long pause. The phone crackled.

"They found him at the caretaker's cottage. He shot himself in the head with a shotgun. Pretty much took it off."

He cleared his throat. "I'm sorry to be the bearer of such news, but I assumed you'd want to know."

I was stunned. I sat for a while, thinking about Boyd and our failed relationship. Again I felt somehow guilty, though I couldn't say why. Suddenly I remembered the unopened package. My hand shook as I slit the brown wrapper and opened the box.

Inside lay two pictures like Dorothea Lange's stark black and white photographs of people during the Depression; a sad-looking middle-aged woman in a flowered housedress and run-over Oxfords, and a man with a miner's cap and sunken cheeks and eyes.

There was a letter inside, too and it took me a while to find the courage to read it.

"Dear Jim," it said.

"I've been writing again and thought you might like to see the stories. If so, I'll send you copies, but you aren't under any obligation either to read them or to answer this. As for these pictures, they are of my family. The woman is my mother and the man is my grandfather.

Boyd."

The letter fell from my hands and I was overcome with guilt and remorse. What if I had opened the package sooner? What if I had answered? Would it have made a difference? Would my few words of friendship have kept him from that desperate act?

All I knew for certain was that I had been ungenerous of spirit, and it would haunt me for the rest of my life.

A BIRTHDAY PARTY

The song has been in Hannah's head all day, darting in and out and hovering like a humming bird. It was there when she awoke, words and music full blown, though she has not thought of it for more than twenty years.

At first she is delighted. She seldom has a chance to speak Polish any more and her native tongue has begun to grow rusty from disuse. Yet now she remembers every word of the plaintive song, a typical tale of love betrayed. Hannah sings it aloud to herself after Bill and the boys leave in the morning.

The trouble is, she can't get it out of her head. As she squeezes the blue icing through the pastry tube, she has to force herself to concentrate. The refrain of the song, "betrayed, betrayed" in it's minor key, makes her feel sad.

Hannah makes these American cakes only for birthdays, preferring the yeast-raised bobka and cream cheese rugelach she remembers from her childhood. Absently humming the refrain, she forms an elaborate circle of rosettes around the edge of the cake and lays the tube on the plate.

As soon as the boys get home, she thinks, I'll have them write the greeting in the center. It will please Bill and involve the kids more in the party.

She pulls a step-stool over so that she can reach the upper oven, glancing out of the window meanwhile to see if the boys are coming.

A small, slim woman with high cheekbones and delicate features, she has round black eyes, shiny, like jet beads.

She has not reminded the boys about Bill's birthday this year. Bill is edgy about turning forty. She doesn't want the boys to dwell on it or joke about it.

Reaching into the oven, she thumps the bread, listening for the hollow thunking sound that means it's done. She draws it out, intensifying the aroma, which co-mingles with the sweet smell of the cake.

Festive. Yes, that's the effect she is after. Earlier in the day she'd set the table with a freshly ironed damask cloth and white candles in silver holders. She'd used her best china and napkins and even her sterling silver place settings.

Yet, the table is set only for four, herself and Bill, David, their oldest son, just turning fifteen and Daniel (her baby, though he would not like to hear her say it) now eleven. It is to be a family party, a happy and special occasion.

It's important for the boys, Hannah thinks. they have seen us quarrel too often. Worse than that, they have endured with me the terrible silences that are Bill's special form of punishment. It we should divorce, they will need happy family memories to sustain them. Absently she hums the refrain of the song.

Happy memories… For a moment she is a little girl again in Poland, before 1939, before the Nazis took her family. She wears a pink dress and a pink hair ribbon and her father is calling from the doorway, "Happy Birthday, Hanela. Come see what we have for you."

Happy memories, she thinks again. Memories that can sustain you through bitter times.

The door slams, bringing Hannah out of her reverie, as the boys burst into the house, laughing and out of breath.

"We could smell the cake from three houses down, mom. I bet David it was coming from our house. Can we have some now?"

Daniel's eyes are a copy of her own.

"No," Hannah says. "It's for tonight. It's a cake for dad's birthday."

"How old is he now?" asks Daniel.

"A year older than last year. Forty."

Hannah tries to say it lightly, off-handedly.

"Look," she says to distract them. "I bought this robe for dad from all of us."

The robe is handsomely tailored in blue velvet, with a small monogram on the pocket.

David laughs, "You arranged it in the box so dad can't miss the label. Givenchy."

He stumbles over the pronunciation. "You want him to know it's expensive."

How bright he is, she thinks. How perceptive. Bill does like quality. I couldn't risk displeasing him.

She gives them the funny card she has bought.

"Write your names above mine," she says and sets them to work wrapping and tying the box.

Simulating a happy mood, she tosses them a roll of crepe paper and a bag of balloons.

"Here, you do the decorating."

David, handsome and dark, bears a striking resemblance to Hannah. Daniel is a composite of both parents, with Bill's fair hair and Hannah's delicate features.

Chattering excitedly, the boys throw the crepe paper across the room to each other, teasing her by skimming it only a foot or two above the china, which they know she cherishes. Surreptitiously, they stick a pin in a balloon. The loud pop almost makes her drop the pot she is holding.

"Stop it," she says. "Behave yourselves." But she laughs as her mood lifts, watching their horseplay, sensing their anticipation.

My family, she thinks. How good it is to have them.

As six o'clock approaches, she sends them, mock protesting, to change their clothes and comb their hair.

"Dad won't recognize us," Daniel insists.

"Yeah," David chimes in. "He'll think he came to the wrong house."

Hannah, too, changes from her slacks into a new ruffled dress in a flowered print, frilly and feminine.

It's a shade too coy and girlish for her thirty-eight years, but she wants nothing sober or matronly this night.

The boys have already inscribed the cake with the blue icing, squeezing elaborate curlicues around the H and B's. Hannah is putting the last candleholder in place as she hears the car door slam. The boys joke and jostle each other, but the air is charged with expectancy.

"Hi," Bill calls from the hall. "Smells good. What's for dinner?"

Hannah stops holding her breath. He's in a good mood, she thinks. It's a good omen. Surreptitiously, wraps her knuckles lightly on the edge of the breadboard.

Without coming into the kitchen, Bill heads down the hall to wash his hands and their suspense grows as they wait to see his reaction when he sees the dining room decorations. He is a long time coming and when he does come, Hannah notes with surprise he has on a fresh shirt and a different tie from the one he wore in the morning. Had he guessed that they were making a party for him? On the threshold, Bill stops, eyeing the table, the decorations.

"What's this?" he says. Her ear catches a sharp note in his voice.

But the boys seem not to notice. "Happy Birthday, Dad," they shout.

Bill nods his thanks. "Why all the fuss?"

Before she can intervene, David says, "Because it's a landmark, Dad. Forty is a landmark."

Oh God, Hannah prays, watching Bill's face darken. Don't let it set him off.

But he says nothing. As they take their seats, Hannah places the elaborately wrapped box in front of him.

"What is it?" he asks.

"A gift from all of us," she says, "but open it after dinner."

"No!" chorus the boys. "Now. Open it now."

Bill tears the paper off and pauses to read the card.

"Come on Dad, open it." Daniel is half standing in his excitement.

Let him like it, Hannah prays silently. Let it be a happy meal.

Bill opens the box and glances at the prominently displayed label. He turns to Hannah sharply, demanding, "Did you charge this?"

"Of course I did." He knows I have no money of my own, she thinks.

"And the dress, too?" he snarls, rising. "You charged that, too, didn't you?" He is shouting, "What the hell kind of present is it, if I have to pay for it myself?"

The boys have grown pale and silent. They stare from Bill to Hannah.

"Bill," she says, "I'm sorry. I thought it would please you. Please, please, can't we go on with the meal? The boys decorated the cake, I…"

"The hell with the meal!" he shouts. "I didn't ask you to make a party. I'm going out."

The boys stand transfixed, unbelieving. Hannah rushes after Bill.

"Wait, Bill," she pleads, but the door opens and closes before she can reach it. She retreats to the kitchen. Not wanting the boys to see the tears she can't control, she turns her back to them. Facing the window, she sees Bill get into the car and drive away.

Suddenly, Hannah realizes that the car had not been parked in the driveway as it usually was, but at the curb.

My God, she thinks, he never intended to stay! He was planning to start an argument all along so he could leave! All that cheeriness when he came in, he was just pretending! The clean shirt. The tie. Yes, she thinks, he's having an affair! She draws in her breath sharply. That's why he was so angry. He felt guilty about the party, about the boys... maybe even about me. But those poor frightened faces didn't hold him in the house.

The song's refrain echoes in her mind. Betrayed, betrayed. I hate him. She has to bit her lips to keep from saying it aloud.

But David is shouting. "I hate him! I hate the son of a bitch!"

Daniel comes to Hannah and puts his arms around her, his beautiful eyes wide and solemn. He doesn't speak but stares at Hannah's face.

She tries to force out the words she has said so many times before, "You must try to understand him." But the words stick in her throat and she begins to cry again.

Now David comes, too and touches her shoulder. Daniel hugs her wordlessly and tries to wipe away her tears with his palm, but David slowly releases her, squares his shoulders and stands a little taller. His voice takes on a new and deeper timbre.

"It's going to be all right, mom," he says. "It's going to be all right."

THE KEYS

Hanna drives the Chevy into the garage and turns off the motor. She slides her small body along the seat until her legs can reach the ground. The heavy two car garage door groans arthritically as she pits her strength against the resistance of its rusty springs. Shoulders sagging, she walks to the rear of the car.

Opening the trunk, she begins lifting out the heavy bags of groceries. The strap of her hand bag slides off her shoulder. Impatiently, she sets down one of the grocery sacks again, slips the strap off her arm, and throws the purse onto the trunk floor. As she lifts the groceries again and puts them down near the kitchen door, her mind recycles the terrible argument she had with Bill the night before.

He'd come home almost an hour late, saying he was delayed at the lab. He ate his dinner quickly, without comment, although she'd made his favorite pot roast. Then he remarked, "I'll have to work all weekend. The experiment isn't going well."

"All weekend?" Hanna asked. "Do you really have to? You promised to take the boys to the ball game! Do they expect you to work that much over-time?"

Bill snapped at her: "Stupid woman! Stop ask-ing questions about things you don't understand."

Once he would have told her not to bother her pretty head about it, but the implication is the same; women in general, and she, in particular, are not bright enough to understand the nature of his work.

They'd had a painful argument. She doesn't want to recall it.

But there is something more. Beyond the supe-riority and contempt is a furtiveness. She senses that he is lying. Another woman? More than likely, and not the first time, either.

Yet, she has no hard proof, nor, as during the other times, does she seek it. In another two or three years, she thinks, when the boys are older, I'll... but the thought trails off, for she doesn't know what she would do, only that in some magical way it would be easier to find a solution.

Balancing the last two bags on her knee, she slams the trunk shut, realizing, an instant too late, that her purse with the car keys is still inside. A wave of anxiety washes over her. What if Bill finds out, she thinks. For a moment she feels weak and faint. She steadies herself, holding onto the car with one hand.

Then she gets the spare house key from the magnetized slot behind the scratched old freezer, lets herself into the kitchen, and begins hauling in the groceries.

Her tension grows, spreading wider, like bubbles in a pot of boiling water. She tries to figure out how she can retrieve her purse without telling Bill what she did. She fears his ridicule. The inability of women to keep in mind two ideas simultaneously was a common theme he used.

He had been so charming once. The thought brings tears to her eyes. Why had he changed? What she done?

She begins to scheme as she does the laundry and prepares dinner. She won't need her car or her purse for the rest of the day. She will say nothing about what happened. But after dinner, when the boys are watching TV and Bill goes in to shower and shave before returning to the lab, she'll go through his trousers. She'll find the car keys, open the trunk, retrieve her purse, and replace his keys before he is out of the bathroom.

Timing, of course, will be critical. Will she be able to get the keys back into his pocket before he comes out of the bathroom? Yes, she decides, there is plenty of time, nothing to worry about.

Bill is brusque as he eats, saying little to any of them, beyond the announcement that he is tired and wants the boys to stop horsing around at the table.

As soon as he is finished, he heads for the bathroom. As she clears the dishes mechanically, she listens with single-minded attention for the sound of the water running in the shower. She waits half a minute to be sure, then walks quickly into the bedroom and lifts his trousers from the chair. She knows the pocket where he keeps his keys. It will take but a minute.

But instead of the keys, her fingers close around a small, square object.

As in a dream, she draws the tiny box out of the pocket and opens it, staring blankly at the diamond solitaire ring, a near twin of her own, that lies inside it. It is neither large nor small, nor in any way remarkable. Her mind registers the physical presence of the ring, and she knows it's not for her. It lies sparkling in her palm, shattering her world, as surely as it's faceted surfaces shatter the light in the room.

She can pretend no longer, and she will have to deal with its consequences, not on her own timetable in some vague future, but here and now. She stands seemingly transfixed, while a volcano of emotions erupts within her. Rage, fear, hurt, uncertainty and a desire for revenge spill over each other in her mind.

Suddenly she is aware that Bill is standing in the room, staring at her, his face so contorted with rage that without realizing it, she raises her hands over her head to protect herself, and the ring falls to the floor.

"How dare you go through my pockets?" Bill shouts. "How dare you!"

Pockets? The keys! Suddenly her timidity and furtiveness seem so ludicrous to her that she begins to laugh and weep at once. In a single sweeping motion, she bends over, retrieves the ring, and flings it in his face.

"How dare I?" She shouts. "How dare you! How dare you lie and cheat and then put me down the way you've done."

Words that surprise her, words that she did not know she would say, pour out of her.

"Get dressed, Bill. Get dressed and go. But don't come back. I'll talk to a lawyer tomorrow and we'll settle things later. But don't say anything now. Don't tell me any more lies."

She turns and starts toward the kitchen, as Bill watches her speechless, ashen, uncertain what to say. Then she turns back, and as he watches, takes the keys from his pocket.

"I need to open the trunk," she says quietly. "I left my purse and my car keys inside it."

TRAIN OF THOUGHT

Diane:

"Usually I like riding on trains. It's nice to relax and look out the window without having to watch the monotonous white line and the in-and out-flowing traffic. I even like the rhythmic sound of the wheels. They put me into an alpha state, and whichever brain lobe it is that does creative thinking takes over.

"I'm not so pleased this time, though, with my fellow traveler across from me in this compartment. He popped in, just as the train was leaving, and it's taken him a while to get settled. A stranger to me, he's somewhere between forty-eight and fifty-five, good-looking in a sort of lop-sided, asymmetrical way. I can feel his eyes staring at me over the edges of his London Times.

"Just what I need, right? What cliche is he going to use? "Lovely day, isn't it? Are you on holiday?" But he doesn't say anything, just keeps on eyeing me in a kind of calculating way.

"It really annoys me. I feel like saying: "Didn't your mother ever teach you that it's rude to gawk at people, mister? I thought the English are supposed to be so polite."

"I glance out the window at the barely undulating plain, with its drab rows of council houses. Taking a last drag on my cigarette, I put it out, but the stranger's examination is really getting to me, so I tap out another one from the pack and light it with the small gold lighter that was a present from Gary on our tenth anniversary. He'd had it engraved D in old English script. I remember him saying that even after ten years, whenever he said my name, it made him think of the hunter goddess, Diane.

"Gary. My ex-husband. I picture him in my mind's eye, the way he looked when we were first married, the long blond hair, that single dimple. How long ago that was. Didn't have my doctorate yet. Wasn't teaching English lit in Boston. Just another suburban mommy. Didn't have a sense of myself then, either. So, if I'm so aware of my self-worth now, I think, why is that idiot across the aisle ogling upsetting me?

"All right, Mac, I tell myself, two can play at the same game. Let's see. You've got on shiny, expensive, Italian shoes, and corduroy trousers, but you've got a sharp crease in them, that's incongruous. Carefully casual, but it's not quite right, somehow. Ok. Now what's on top? Harris tweed jacket with suede elbow patches, and a black turtle-neck sweater. Professorial clothes. Don at Oxford? Something (the Italian shoes maybe, or the sharp crease) isn't quite English.

"I puff on my cigarette and realize that he's staring at me again. Wondering if my makeup is smeared, I try to catch a glimpse of my reflection in the window. When I look back, our eyes meet. Well, I think, if you can't beat 'em… So, I give him a s sort of half smile. Which he doesn't return. In some chagrin, I turn back to the window again. Well, Mr. Tweed Jacket, I say to myself, what kind of game are you playing?

"The train stops at a small suburban station. Cookie-cutter, carbon-copy commuters, I think, as I watch the line of briefcase-laden men in their pin-stripe suits and rolled "brollies" get off, to be greeted by jeans-clad women and tow-headed offspring. The scene isn't too different from any suburban station in the States, except for the school uniforms on the small children.

"A portly man in a bowler hat rattles past the door of the compartment as the train starts again. The man in the tweed jacket rustles his newspaper, turning the pages noisily. Irritating creep, I think, as I look out the window.

"We both glance up as a fat woman in a ridiculous hat that looks like a tired salad starts to enter the compartment. I guess I'm still glaring, because she beats a hasty retreat back out into the corridor.

"I peer out the window again. The scenery is still unremarkable, but more pleasant. Gently rolling grassy fields, demarcated by old hedgerows flash by, dotted with sheep, like pictures on a calendar.

"Out of boredom, I look at the man with the newspaper again. Definitely a professional man, I decide. His nails are neatly manicured, and his hands show no signs of hard labor. Something about his hands, the squareness of the fingertips, perhaps, reminds me of my son. Allen's in medical school now, has another year to go before his Residency. It's comforting to know that he's well launched, though it has strained my professor's salary rather severely at times to get him through. How I hated all those hamburgers.

"I've had precious little help from Gary, God knows. He's a lawyer and doing well, and he turns up, sporadically, with a check for Madelaine's tuition at Vassar, or Allen's books, but I can't count on it. Every once in a while, his conscience begins to hurt, and that's when the checks come. I don't hold my breath for them, though. Well, he has another family now. I've managed without him for the most part. It give me a certain satisfaction.

"I check out the view again. It's getting late, and the train is casting long moving shadows. I look back at my travel companion, at the Harris tweed jacket. I imagine it smelling pleasantly of fragrant pipe tobacco. An old familiar feeling creeps over me.

"To calm myself, I turn back toward the window, and glance at my watch. Almost there, I think, relieved.

"Looking a my fellow traveler again, I imagine the man smell clinging to the woolen sweater. I think of what it would be like if he held me close: the scratchy feel of the jacket and the sweater, the smooth feel of flesh beneath them. I try to remember what it felt like to be in love.

"Stop it, I tell myself! Cut it out now! You're not a heroine in a nineteenth century novel. You're a strong, independent woman. If you want to climb into bed with a man, do it, but don't go off on any romantic dream of being a clinging vine in a country cottage.

"Dusk is falling, and I can hardly see out the window any more. The man has snapped on the overhead light. His face, in high relief, seems more rugged and handsome than before.

"I imagine how the skin would feel under my fingers, imagine kissing those strong lips, imagine, *no, no imagining,* I tell myself. I've got enough to do to complete my book before my grant runs out. I don't need any entanglements, not with you, not with any-one. Even a one night stand means drinks, chit-chat, exchanges of identities, because somehow, we hu-mans can't seem to just have a roll in the hay with someone and no names, thank you. No, I haven't time for all that.

"When the train gets to Oxford, I'll see Professor Corwin, concerning the special archives he wrote me about. Then I'll have a hot bath, and get to bed early. Tomorrow I'll spend the day at the library, researching. With any luck, I'll get my grant check from that Synchron Company businessman quickly, and not have to waste a lot of time. I don't need you, Mr. Tweed Jacket. I don't need anyone like you.

"'I want a cigarette badly, but it's gone out, and I rummage in my bag for a fresh one and my lighter. I've got to stop smoking.

"Professor Corwin. What will he be like, I wonder? Dry, desiccated? Handsome, virile? No, I tell myself, *no*.

"I look out the window again, but there's nothing to see. Darkness has descended completely."

Bill:

"The woman who sits opposite me in the compartment of the train from London to Oxford is no spring chicken. Fortyish, I'd guess. Good looking broad, though, smartly dressed, nicely coifed. Blonde hair. Real or dyed? Hard to tell. Hatless, anyway.

Unusual for an Englishwoman. They do affect the most awful headgear.

"I guess she realizes I'm looking at her over the edge of my paper, because she turns sort of deliberately and stares out the window.

"She's puffing on a cigarette, and I curse myself for getting to the train so late that I couldn't find a non-smoking compartment. I think of asking her not to smoke. I hate cigarettes, and I think women look awfully coarse blowing out smoke. But, of course, I'm the one in the wrong car, and she's just putting it out, anyway, so I don't say anything.

"After a minute, though, she finds a fresh one, Eve, isn't that an American brand? She lights it with a small gold lighter marked D, as far as I can tell, in old English script. Dorothy? I wonder. Diane? Debra?

"She glances over at me, sort of down at my shoes and pants, and frowns slightly. Did I put the wrong clothes combination together? What's bugging her, anyway?

"The English are funny about things like that. Like yesterday, at the breakfast meeting with Johnston, when I put some marmalade on my toast and ate it with my bacon. He had the queerest look, so I asked him if something was wrong and he said, "A sweet with a savory?" as if I'd done something terribly gauche.

"Well, that remark is going to cost the supercilious bastard. If he can't be tactful with me, knowing I'm the VP at Syncron and looking him over for plant manager, he won't be any good with customers or staff, either.

"The woman is still sort of appraising me. She looks carefully at my jacket and sweater, and puffs on that damned cigarette. What's the matter, lady haven't you ever seen an American before?

"So, I stare back at her, and she turns to look out the window, but all of a sudden, she looks back and our eyes meet. She gives me an odd sort of tentative smile.

"Forget it lady, I think. When I get to Oxford, I have enough work ahead of me to choke a horse. Not to mention that lady writer I have to meet. That's going to take a while, too. I can't just hand her the money and go. I'll have to report to Tom on what kind of progress she's making. I don't know why he didn't handle this nonsense himself. The Foundation and the grant was his idea.

"Anyway, the last thing I need is a little romantic fling. She sure is a good looking woman, though, with those big brown eyes, and those high cheekbones.

"All of a sudden I'm thinking about my wife, Edith, back in Scarsdale, and I feel uncomfortable, sort of guilty. And I haven't done a damn thing! I've never cheated on Edith but I know our marriage is falling apart. In a year or two, when the last of the children is gone, maybe...

"Anyway, I don't smile back at the blonde. Instead, I gaze out the window. I can see a monotonous line of hedgerows separating the fields. Someone, Johnston maybe, told me the other day, that they were hundreds of years old. In the States, the developers would have torn them out by now.

"The train stops jerkily, and I watch the passengers dismount: mostly commuters in dark pinstripes and carrying umbrellas. Oddly, there are no bowler hats like the ones you always see in British movies. The style must have changed, I guess.

"I turn the pages of my newspaper to the stock quotations, but the paper catches an air pocket and I have to bang it shut. I try to do it as quietly as I can but the woman opposite me frowns, I suppose be-cause of the noise. Tit for tat, lady, I think. It's better than that crummy cigarette smoke.

"The blonde is staring out the window again. A stout woman in a froufrou cabbage rose hat starts to enter our compartment. The blonde and I both look up, and I'm about to move my briefcase off the seat to make room for the fat lady, when all of a sudden she backs out again. Good riddance. One woman, in here with cigarettes is enough!

"Suddenly, the woman turns from the window and stares straight at me, cool as a cucumber. She looks at my hands, my face, my sweater, my jacket. Is she seriously interested? She has nice legs, long and shapely. The breasts aren't bad either, and just faintly, against the blue angora sweater, I can make out the tips of her nipples.

"I can feel the juices begin to flow, and a familiar stirring. Feeling a bit embarrassed, I lower the news-paper so that it covers me from the waist down. I haven't slept with Edith for three weeks. I'm not a kid anymore, pushing fifty, but I'm not dead, either. Three weeks without, and a good looking broad who might be willing... well, I think of Edith again, Edith and her causes and her earnestness. Then I think of my daughter, Vickie, working in the lab in Boston. And I think of the other kids still in school.

"No one would know, of course. Still, it would take a whole lot of time, entanglement. She doesn't look like a one-night stand. And time is one thing I don't have to spare right now. After the meetings at Oxford, I'll have to get right back to London to supervise the opening of the new branch.

"I feel a cold chill of regret, and a sort of shriveling inside. Good looking woman. Too bad, really. I snap on the reading light. 'She's lit another cigarette. I couldn't have put up with the smoking anyway, I tell myself. Probably just as well. I look out the window again, surprised to see that it's grown completely dark outside."

A LAW ABIDING WOMAN

Agnes Warner peers through the peephole in her front door at a handsome blond young man with a short haircut.

"Yes", she asks, "What is it?"

The man holds a badge up close to the peephole and what appears to be an ID card. "Fire Department, ma'm," he says, "making a routine inspection for frayed cords and other hazards. May I come in?"

Mrs. Warner, a small graying woman of sixty-three, counters, "Routine? Nobody ever came here before for an inspection program like that." Her life has been uneventful. Mrs. Warner intends to keep it that way.

Patiently, the man answers, "It's a new program, ma'm, and we won't come in without your permission. I'll put a flyer through your mail slot and you can read it."

The flyer indicates a neighborhood survey sponsored by the fire department. Almost satisfied, Mrs. Warner opens the door a crack and peruses the man from head to velcro-fastened jogging shoes. He is neatly, even conservatively, dressed in tan sweater and trousers, and his smile is boyishly appealing.

"Maybe I can talk to your husband about the program, ma'm?" It is a question. He makes no attempt to come inside.

"I'm a widow," Mrs. Warner answers, and could have bitten off her tongue.

"Well then, you can follow me as I make my inspection, and I'll show you any hazards I find" he says authoritatively.

She closes the door, but stands near it, instead of following the man as he begins to examine the lamps in the living room. Wordlessly he inspects two lamp cords. Examining a third, he whistles sharply. "Look at this, ma'm. You could have had a fire anytime." Crouching, cord in hand, he beckons her and she comes to look at it.

As she stoops forward, he turns and half rises, catching her off balance and knocking her to the floor with a swift motion of his hands and shoulders.

Stunned, Mrs. Warner tries to scream, but instantly he is on top of her, his left hand clamping her mouth shut. With his right hand, he put the blade of a large knife just below the lobe of her left ear. Part of her mind registers that it is warm, as though it had been next to his body. She is afraid to move.

"That's fine," says the man smiling. "Just cooperate and everything will be ok. I'm going to put a piece of tape over your mouth now. Don't try to scream. The knife is sharp." He nicks her very lightly with the point, and she feels something wet on her neck.

Removing his hand, he slaps a piece of tape across her mouth. Then, pinning her down with his left hand and using the knife with his right, he cuts away some of her clothing swiftly and expertly, as though he has done it before. "I want you to keep your eyes open," he says.

Smiling, he rapes her, brutally, painfully, his eyes never leaving her face.

When he is spent, he yanks her by both arms to a chair, pulls a length of rope from his pocket, and ties her, hands and feet, to the chair. Knife in hand, he spends another few minutes dumping and ransacking the contents of drawers, her jewelry box and her purse.

Then he turns to her, laughing. "I'm leaving now, er…" He looks at the driver's license he has shaken from her purse… "Agnes. Thanks for everything." He makes a sweeping gesture that includes her and the house. "You've been very generous, Aggie," he says, "Now, one more thing. Don't call the police or notify anyone else about this. Otherwise…" he glances briefly at the knife, "I might have to come back sometime."

For a long time after he leaves, she sits in the chair as though turned to stone. She makes no attempt to free herself. Finally she begins to feel cold to the depths of her being. She shudders repeatedly and struggles to remove the ropes from her hands and feet, as, mouth still taped, she fights an urge to retch. At last she is free and she goes at once to the bathroom and showers for a long long time. She puts on fresh clothing, throws all of the clothes she had been wearing into the trash can and washes her hands again and again.

But she calls no one. She is ashamed to tell her daughter, or her friends, afraid to face the police and their accusing questions. She has locks installed on all her windows, dead-bolts on the doors. For the first time in her life, fear is her regular companion. In her mind she relives the incident again and again. With each replay, her hatred of the man grows, until it is almost a tangible thing.

Increasingly, she curtails her activities, going out only when it is an absolute necessity, opening the door only when she is certain of her visitor. In time, she becomes almost a recluse, so that when the summons for jury duty comes, three years later, she is terribly dismayed. The thought of coming home alone after dark makes her tremble. What if he comes back while I'm gone and waits in the house, she thinks.

Repeatedly, she reads the list of excuses from duty, but can find nothing that applies.

She has been going to the jury room for three days now, and her panel, which has been assigned to traffic court, has been called only once. It is a routine accident case and the jurors are selected quickly, in alphabetical order, long before Mrs.

Warner can be called. She and the rest of her panel are dismissed from the case and sent back to the jury room to await another call.

There is little to do and she watches the other potential jurors kill time playing cards, gossiping and reading. A small stirring of life comes back to her. I'm hungry for the sound of human voices, she thinks. He's robbed me of that, too.

A stout woman drops out of a gin game, and Mrs. Warner is invited to join. She plays animatedly as the afternoon drones on, enjoying the almost forgotten pleasure of being with people again.

Suddenly there is a flurry of activity. Several panels are called, including hers. This time, however, the panel has been reassigned to criminal courts. Even the name "criminal" brings a rush of loathing. Mrs. Warner does not want to deal with criminals ever again.

In the courtroom, facing the judge, sit the accused and his lawyer. Mrs. Warner can see only his back, but her heart gives a sudden lurch. She fights panic. Controlling her breathing carefully so that she will not retch, she reasons with herself. No, it can't be. Get hold of yourself, Agnes. You're getting paranoid. Lots of people look alike from the rear.

Quickly the judge administers the oath to the panel. In a routine, dispassionate manner he outlines the nature of the case.

"The young man at the table, whose name is….." He glances at a paper, "William Martin, is accused of raping and robbing a woman. I estimate that the case will take about three weeks, since most of the jury has already been chosen from a previous panel. If anyone on the present panel feels that he or she cannot serve due to the length of the case, or for any other reason, would you raise your hand and explain and I'll consider whether to excuse you."

Mrs. Warner is in a turmoil. She does not want to sit as a juror in a rape case, raking up all the old terror again. But what reason can I give, she asks herself. I can't plead the pressure of time. I can't tell the judge and all these people my secret. Maybe I won't be called. Maybe the jury will be filled before they come to the W's and the panel will be dismissed again.

But the judge announces in a droning voice that potential jurors will be called in reverse alphabetical order, starting with Z. Mrs. Warner barely has time to digest this when suddenly the accused turns and looks carefully at the panel. Simultaneously, William Martin and Agnes Warner recognize each other.

For a wild moment, Mrs. Warner wants only to run away, to hide. Again she feels nauseated. Then a great wave of rage sweeps over her. I want to see him dead, she thinks.

Meanwhile, the color has drained from William Martin's face. He hesitates, then turns and whispers something to his attorney. The older man looks up and back at the panel. There is a whispered, but obviously heated exchange between the accused and his attorney. Then William Martin shakes his head from side to side.

The flurry of activity has not escaped the judge. "Mr. Kasper," he says to William Martin's attorney, "Is something wrong? Does your client recognize someone on the panel?"

The attorney glances briefly at his client, but he only says, "No, your Honor."

The judge persists. "Mr. Kasper, I want to remind you that you have already exhausted your peremptory challenges. You're sure?"

Mr. Kasper glances at his client again. "Your Honor," he says, "may we have a very brief recess?"

"Very well, I'll give you ten minutes. Those who wish to smoke may do so in the corridor, but please be back in ten minutes."

When everyone has reassembled, the judge asks, "Well Mr. Kasper?"

"We're ready, your Honor."

"Mrs. Helena Zubretsky," calls the clerk. A tall angular woman steps forward.

"Mrs. Zubretseky," says Mr. Kasper, "have you ever known anyone who was raped?"

"No, I mean, no sir," she replies, rubbing her palms against her skirt.

"We all know that rape is an emotional subject," Mr. Kasper says. "Now, Mrs. Zubretsky, the law states that you must disqualify yourself if you cannot render a fair and impartial verdict. Remember that you are under oath. Is there any reason why you would not be able to do so?"

"No sir."

"Acceptable," Mr. Kasper tells the judge and Mrs. Zubretsky is seated on the jury.

The clerk calls, "Mr. Henry Washington." A small balding black man comes forward briskly.

"You are a restaurant cook, Mr. Washington?" asks the lawyer, looking at a file card.

"Yes sir."

"You meet a lot of people on the job, I presume. Ever know anyone involved in a rape?"

"No sir. Cooks don't do the sociable part."

A small ripple of laughter goes through the courtroom.

The judge glances at his watch. "Do you think we can get on with this, Mr. Kasper?"

"Of course, your Honor."

"Mr. Washington, is there any reason why you could not render a fair and impartial verdict?"

"Not that I know of," Mr. Washington replies.

"Accepted."

Except for the alternates, there remains one seat to fill.

"Mrs. Agnes Warner," calls the clerk.

Knees shaking, Mrs. Warner takes her seat.

"Mrs. Warner," says the attorney, "have you any daughters?"

"One," she replies.

"Speak up please," says the judge.

"Would that influence your verdict?" Mr. Kasper asks.

"No sir," she says, raising her voice, and shifts in her seat so that she is facing the accused.

"Is there any reason…" begins the attorney.

"Mr. Kasper," interjects the judge, "I have already sworn the panel. Is this repetition necessary?"

"Please bear with me, your Honor. I have my reasons."

The judge looks at his watch pointedly.

"All right, go on."

Mr. Kasper is a bit flustered.

"Is there any reason why you cannot render a fair verdict?" he asks. He has left out the word "impartial". Before she can answer, he adds a coda. "A simple yes or no will do."

The law-abiding habits of a life-time crowd in on Agnes Warner. She hesitates. Then she looks squarely at William Martin. Firmly she replies, "No sir. No reason at all."

A STRANGER AT MY DOOR

Hal and I had been married for three years when the problem first came up. I don't know why we hadn't discussed it sooner. I guess each of us had just assumed our partner's attitude.

Of course, we were both wrong, very wrong. I wanted children; Hal didn't. It was a fundamental difference, and talking and counseling didn't change it. And so we divorced.

Then on a Tuesday morning I'll never forget, I opened the front door to leave for work and almost tripped over a cardboard box with a baby inside! The child was wrapped in a pink and white blanket, and a pillow had been place underneath it. There was even a bottle of formula and a package of Similac, placed at the baby's feet. Whoever had abandoned the child had loved it, I was sure.

My first instinct was to pick up the box, take the baby into the house, and keep it forever. I even looked up and down the street to be sure that no one had seen me lifting it. I could feel adrenaline pumping. Suppose I didn't report it. Suppose I just told the neighbors I'd adopted the child. Would they believe me? Would they report me for kidnapping? What was the penalty for not reporting a found baby?

I picked up the now crying infant and un-wrapped the blanket and diaper. She was a beautiful little girl, well formed, with a fuzz of dark curly hair. I held the formula bottle for her, while I dialed my office and called in sick. When the baby's little fingers curled around mine, I knew I couldn't give her up.

I wrestled with the problem for several hours, meanwhile tending the little girl and rocking her in my arms. Who was the mother? Would she come back and demand the child?

After a while, common sense weighed in. I didn't have the money to pay for a full time baby sitter, and I needed to work to survive. Alone, without a husband or boyfriend, or even someone to share expenses, there was no way I could keep the little girl, whom I had already named April in my head.

Hands shaking, I held the baby close for a minute, and then put her back in the box. Slowly and reluctantly, I dialed the police. "Hello," I said, "I want…" I hesitated for a second. "I want to report an abandoned child."

EMPTY NEST

Robert taught her how to use the gun, how long
ago? Ages, eons. Just after he came home from the
war, it was. Funny, she thinks, to the kids it's ancient
history, World War II, like the Civil War or the Revolution.

Janice feels the old German Luger, heavy and
awkward in her hand, like a new golf club or an un-
familiar pot. She hasn't held it for years. For a while
she'd kept it by the bedside, the way Robert had
wanted, but after the kids came, (God! Eileen, the
baby has just gone off to college!) she was afraid to
have it around and she put it away at the top of her
closet. Forgotten: until now.

She can feel the safety catch behind the dull
metallic barrel. Though the gun hasn't been used in
years, the clip came right out this morning. She
loaded it with six bullets from the box and put the
clip back in.

Now she balances it in her hand and her index
finger curls on the trigger. She imagines a target, the

way he had showed her, and she points it squarely at the back of Robert's head.

"Is that you, Hon?" Robert doesn't turn his head.

His voice unnerves her and she lowers the gun but keeps it cradled in her palm.

"Be through grading papers in ten minutes. Can it wait?"

"No, it can't wait," she says. "It's waited too long already." Her voice is low, mechanical. "It's waited five years: waited for Paul and Janey and Eileen to go off to school."

He turns quickly, the lamplight creating a faint halo behind his head, making him look like a saint on a Russian icon. His eyes widen and he starts to rise. "Janice, what..."

The gun comes up again. "It's waited through the tramp at the book store and the redhead in the tight skirts and all the little opportunists who wanted an A. No, it can't wait any more." Her voice cracks. "It can't wait anymore at all."

He takes a step forward. "Jan, put it down. It isn't loaded. It wouldn't fire anyway. It hasn't been used in years. Let's talk."

"Try it," she says. "Keep coming."

His eyes search for cover. "They didn't mean anything to me, Jan. It's you I love. You know that. But you were so busy with the kids. I felt, I don't know, shut out, unimportant. Janice, for God's sake, please put it down before it goes off."

"I wouldn't have minded so much if they had mattered to you, your tramps and Lolitas." Her voice is rising. "They made me feel cheap, soiled." Tears stream down her face, and with her left hand she rubs at them.

"It's been five years, Jan." His voice is careful, controlled. "Why now?"

"Because I don't need the nest any more, that's why. The birds have flown."

"But how could you pretend for so long that you didn't know, that nothing was wrong?"

"I had a very good teacher." She laughs bitterly. "Notice the past tense, Robert. She aims the gun directly at his heart. "I <u>had</u> a very good teacher."

PROMISED JOY

When I awoke that summer morning I was smiling. I knew the day would be memorable, one of the happiest of my life. Patti, our youngest daughter was getting married, and her husband-to-be was the son of our dearest friend.

We'd known Rob since he was born, and a kinder, sweeter, warmer person I've never known. He was every girl's dream husband, too, with his dark, sheik of Arby good looks, and a great sense of humor. Already, at twenty-seven, he had a thriving medical practice, but he was not one of those pedantic types who bore you at parties with their self-centered talk. No, Rob was a real Renaissance man, interested in art and music, science and sports. We loved him like a son.

Patti had gone a different route. She'd reached sixteen at the end of the sixties, the time of the flower children, when everything was in flux and all the societal rules were changing. My husband, Dan, and I, are not prudes and we tried to give her plenty of leeway, but Patti was really pushing the envelope. She was such a pretty girl, with her long dark hair and mischievous black eyes, but she'd turn up barefooted in these rag-bag clothes she'd bought at the Good Will store. She'd gotten herself a tattoo of a blue butterfly up on her right shoulder, and even though she was pretty well endowed, she wouldn't wear a bra. We knew we shouldn't pass judgement on her, but it was embarrassing for us when friends and family gathered.

Then, Patti joined a commune for two years, and became involved with drugs and casual sex. She was our youngest, our flower, bright and sharp-witted, and it broke our hearts.

After a while, she left the commune and took up with a ne'er-do-well young man, slight and thin and ill-looking, who could barely read and couldn't hold a job and drank six-packs of beer in lieu of meals. He depended on Patti for everything, and she took a job in a bookstore and was supporting them both. Then, suddenly, to our surprise, she started college, and after a year, she left the young man.

She came back home on a visit after that, and we could see she'd changed. She was wearing attractive sports clothes again, and she'd had her hair styled.

That biting, hurtful edge to her humor was gone. She was back to being the warm, loving daughter we'd always known.

She'd known Rob, all of her life, of course, but suddenly, they were seeing each other with new eyes. Within four months of that visit, they told us they were getting married. Annette, Rob's mother, and I, literally cried on each other's shoulders with happiness.

Patti and Rob decided on an unconventional wedding, out under the live-oak trees in a park just north of San Fernando Valley. They arranged a special gourmet caterer, and as a joke, Patti had the whole second tier of the wedding cake decorated with copies of her butterfly tattoo. She'd had her grandmother's wedding dress altered to fit. I cried again when I saw her in that white lace dress. She was so beautiful.

Dan and I were driving up from LA to the park for the wedding, and the traffic was moving very slowly. We'd given ourselves plenty of time, but still I was annoyed. I wanted to help Patti check out the arrangements. She and Rob had gone about a half hour ahead of us. Because the cake was made by a special bakery, they'd taken it with them in the van.

Finally we reached the cause of the slowdown. There'd been an accident up ahead, three cars slammed together and terribly mangled. There was a tow truck in the right lane, and an ambulance, and the were using the jaws of life device.

My husband, Dan, began pulling over to the shoulder. He's a doctor, and I knew he wanted to help out, but selfishly I thought, just this once, on Patti's wedding day, couldn't we leave it to someone else?

Our car slowed to a stop, and we got out, just as the tow truck pulled the first car out of the traffic lane, and what I saw made my blood freeze. There in the roadway, where the tow truck had been, lay a wedding cake, smashed and dirty, but still recognizable, with the little bride and groom still intact at the top, and on the second tier, a circle of crushed blue butterflies. Though Dan and I ran to the mangled cars, I knew in my heart what had happened. A weight such as I'd never know settled itself on my heart.

Patti was buried in the wedding gown and Rob in the tuxedo just three days after the accident. I kept thinking of how I'd awakened with a smile on the morning of the wedding, and all the joy I'd anticipated. A verse from Robert Burns kept echoing in my head:

"The best laid schemes o' mice and men
Gang oft a-gley
And lea'e us nought but grief an pain
For promised joy."

I wept for Patti and Rob, and Annette, and Dan, and for myself, and the loss of that "promised joy". I wanted to go back to that sunny morning before the accident, and freeze that moment forever.

JOYRIDE

I'm seventeen years old and I'm sitting here in jail in this crummy jumpsuit that makes me look like I'm pregnant. I've got like about a zillion charges hanging over my head, and all I did was borrow a car to go joyriding.

This jerk had left his BMW at the curb, with the motor running, and the keys in the ignition. In that neighborhood, I figured he'd be lucky if I took the car, because otherwise it would have been stripped clean in two minutes.

I was just going to use it till the gas ran out, and then leave it, but the guy reports it stolen, and all hell breaks out. I haven't gone three blocks, when I hear the sirens screaming, and see the blue lights flashing. There's at least three of them.

I don't want no jail time, so I jam my foot on the accelerator, and take off flying. I figured the cops, with their crummy Fords, will never be able to catch up with this souped-up BMW.

Next thing I know, there's two more cop cars on my ass, so I hightail it to the 405 Freeway, with the accelerator on the floor. I'm doing a hundred or more, and I'm having to change lanes all the time, because the moron drivers ahead of me won't get out of the way. My heart's banging, and I can feel a rush, a high, like you get with a speed fix.

So now a helicopter joins the chase, and he's picking me out with his searchlights. I figure I better get off the Freeway, and circle back to my old neighborhood. I'll ditch the car, run up an alley, and over some backyard fences, and I'm home free.

When I hit the street, though, there are all these shit- heads stopped for a light. I pull out around them, floor the accelerator again, and run the red light. A big old van comes out of nowhere from the side street. I jerk the wheel to the left, and miss the van by inches. It must have swerved, too because it spun out, and hit a hydrant. (I only found that out later, and that it was loaded with eight little kids from something called "The Wee Care").

The cops are still behind me, but they're slowing down a little. I turn a corner, and nearly off a guy who's crossing the street. I swing around him, and smack head on into a pickup that's coming the other way. Crunch! That BMW's an accordion.

Both my doors are stuck. There's glass every-where. I'm bleeding all over. The cops get me out with this Jaws of Life thing, but it takes the idiots at least a half hour till they're able to do it. I can see the guy in the pickup and he ain't moving. I don't know if he's dead or what.

The pigs stick cuffs on me before they even let the paramedics take me to the hospital. They put a cop outside the door while I'm being examined, like I'm gonna run with the way I'm banged up. Got a busted knee, and a collapsed lung. The worst thing is, I've got all these cuts on my face, and I don't know if they'll leave scars.

The medics stitch me up, and in a couple of days I end up booked into this jail. They give me a lawyer, but I think he's straight out of law school, and the moron says I better cop a plea to involuntary man-slaughter, stealing a car, reckless driving, and driving without a license. I only borrowed the car, for Christ's sake. I didn't mean to smash it up, or to kill the guy in the pickup.

I don't know. If I plea bargain, I'll still have to do plenty of time, but the jerk lawyer says otherwise they're going to hang me out to dry, and they've got me dead to rights and all.

Funny things is, that stupid jerk, who left the BMW's motor running, is a hot-shot lawyer from uptown. He was down in the 'hood to buy some crack. Went to report the car stolen, and the cops frisked him, because what was he doing in that neighborhood anyway, and with the motor running?

They found the crack on him, and some other stuff, too, so they booked him. He's out on bail, of course, but being a big shot, I bet he gets away with no jail time at all. Meanwhile, I sit here, and like I said, I only meant to borrow the fuckin' car.

ELEVATOR

It's funny, but I almost didn't take that elevator. I'd been out shopping that morning. I was all dressed up in a pink suit and matching pumps, and I'd just had a new hairdo the day before.

I was supposed to meet two of my friends for lunch at a Chinese restaurant on 53rd Street in half an hour, but crossing Madison, I had to dodge one of Manhattan's crazy taxi drivers and somehow popped a big run in my pantyhose. I had just bought three pairs at Bloomingdales' and I was only two blocks from my husband's high-rise office, so I decided to go there first to change my hose.

The building is one of those older 1920's art deco structures with an elaborate marble lobby and twelve elevator entrances decorated with fancy gilded bronze scrolls, with arrows telling which floor the cars are on.

I'd pressed the button and when the elevator arrived, I was about to enter. Suddenly a small, silver-haired woman, garbed in an expensive, understated grey silk dress, the kind that wealthy older women wear, crossed hurriedly from the opposite bank of elevators. She was pushing a man in a wheelchair, so I stepped aside and let them enter ahead of me.

The man appeared to be asleep. He wore a grey houndstooth-check cap and his head was slumped down, so that I couldn't see his face. His lap was covered by a plaid throw. I assumed that they were going to one of the doctor's offices in the building.

The elevator was fairly narrow. It had been mirrored on three sides to make it seem more spacious, but I knew from experience that ordinarily even five people would have been a pretty tight fit, so with the wheelchair taking up so much space, I considered waiting for the next one.

I glanced at my watch, realized that I didn't have much time, so I entered.

Just as the doors were closing, a man with a briefcase scooted in. He was over six feet tall, balding and a bit paunchy. I guessed that he had been running, because his face was red and his brow was sweaty and he was breathing rather hard.

Having the three of us and the wheelchair squeezed in like that made me feel a bit claustrophobic, but since it was a high-speed elevator and I was only going to the forty-ninth floor I figured I could stand it for a minute or so.

The tall man was nearest the buttons and he punched in seventy-nine. His hands were huge, like a basketball players. The silver-haired woman spoke for the first time. "Forty-seven please."

Her voice was higher-pitched than I expected and her pronunciation a bit coarser. I decided that she was either prematurely grey or had had a face lift.

"Forty-nine for me, please." I said.

Nobody spoke as we passed the twentieth and then the thirtieth floor. I was checking myself out in the mirror and thinking I looked pretty good for thirty-six years. No movie star, but not bad, either. My new hair-do showed my black hair to perfection and the new shade of eye-shadow made my eyes look violet.

Then, just as the arrows showed half way between the thirty-eighth and thirty-ninth floor, the car suddenly stopped. It didn't lurch or jerk, just stopped dead and the lights went out. A little red light came on near the emergency button. I guess it was on a different power source.

We all sort of looked at each other in that dim light, but nobody spoke for about twenty seconds. I suppose all of us assumed the power would come on right away, but after about a minute, the grey-haired woman, who looked panicky, bleated, "What do you think we should do?"

"Don't get upset," the tall man said. "It might be just a temporary outage."

He pressed the red button and picked up the phone.

"Security," came a voice. "What's the problem?"

"You tell us." The big man's voice seemed irritable. "We're stuck up here between thirty-eight and thirty-nine. It there a power outage?"

"No," the voice said. "My control panel doesn't show you stuck. It says you're just past fiftieth and moving."

"I don't care what it says." The man sounded really angry. "I tell you we're stuck, and the lights are out."

"All right, all right. Don't panic." The disembodied voice was unnerving. "I'll check it out and get right back to you. You're sure you're stuck?"

"Would I make it up?" The big man's voice was sarcastic.

At least a minute and a half had passed and we were all getting nervous.

"You think we're going to get out of this ok?" The woman's voice quavered.

"Stop it, Marie!" It was the first time the guy in the wheelchair spoke and his tone was sharp. "Calm down."

It was more of an order than a suggestion.

Marie sort of whimpered, "But what if…?"

The phone crackled, but the voice was garbled.

"What?" The man with the briefcase asked.

"Ergulcy groom," said the voice through the static. And then more clearly, "Police coming."

I was really frightened. Why were the police coming? Or did he say Security police? Shouldn't he have called the emergency crew or the fire department or the rescue squad? What if we lost touch with Security completely? How were we going to get out? Was there enough air? I could feel the sweat breaking out and I was getting more claustrophobic by the minute.

At the mention of the police, Marie turned pale.

"Scotty," she yelled, "we've got to get out of here."

And then the damnedest thing happened! The wheelchair guy stood up! The plaid shawl fell to the floor and so did a gun he must have been hiding under it.

The tall man was fiddling with his briefcase straps. He made a dive for the gun, but Scotty scooped it up and ordered him to get back. I was surprised to see that he was much younger than I'd thought and had a big scar across his cheek. He seemed very agile for a sick guy. In fact he didn't seem ill at all. Holding the gun, he pushed the wheelchair to the center of the car.

"What are you going to do?" Marie whined. "What if the police...?"

"Shut up!" Scotty snarled.

He made sure the wheelchair brake was on. Then he climbed up on it and felt around the car's ceiling for the loose panel near the light bulb. Sliding it back, he pulled himself up onto the roof of the elevator car. I looked up and saw steel cables that seemed to stretch endlessly. I almost fainted.

"Get up on the chair," the man ordered Marie. "Hurry up! It's only half a floor. We'll climb out."

She scrambled up on the wheelchair like a gazelle, but sort of whimpering the whole time. Scotty reached down and began to haul her up.

Something grey slithered to the floor and at first I thought it was a rat and my heart pumped adrenaline like crazy. But it didn't move and then I saw it was a wig and as Marie disappeared onto the car roof, I could see that she was a blonde and young.

I turned to the tall man. "Should we climb out, too?" I was shaking so much I could hardly get the words out.

"No," the big guy said. "If the power comes on before they make it to the floor, they're goners. But they're afraid of the police. Didn't you see?"

I nodded. I just couldn't talk.

The big guy lifted the phone again. Security came right on.

"We're right on it. Hang in there. We should have the power on in a minute."

"No! Wait!" the big guy shouted. "Two of the people climbed out through the ceiling panel. They're trying to shinny up the cable to the thirty-ninth. For

God's sake, don't turn the power on yet. You'll kill them."

"Shit!" the security man said and then all of a sudden there was a little hum and the car jerked up a little bit and Marie came tumbling back into the car.

"Scotty's on the cable!" she screamed. "Don't let them turn the power on."

"Tell him to climb down to the car carefully." Security said. "Tell him there's no way he can open the door to the floor. It's automatic. It won't open till the elevator gets there. He can't pry it open. Tell him, as soon as he gets back in the car, we'll get the current back on."

"Scotty," Marie screamed. "You can't get out that way. Security says the door won't open and the power's about to come on. Come back down, for God's sake."

I noticed that her leg was bleeding, but she didn't pay any attention to it.

"Scotty, I don't care about the police. You'll get killed. Please, please come down."

We heard a thud on the roof of the car and then Scotty's feet swung through the hole. He made a sort of "oof" sound as his feet hit the seat of the wheel-chair hard.

Once he was down, he pushed the wheelchair back into the corner, sat down, and put the cap back on and pulled the shawl over his lap. But he held the gun up under it and pointed it at us.

"Nobody knows who tried to get out, so just shut your faces when we reach the floor and everything will be fine."

Marie was scrambling around on the floor, picking up her wig. She put it on and adjusted it as she looked into the mirror. It was a little the worse for wear and frantically she tucked the ends in.

Meanwhile the briefcase guy had picked up the phone again.

"Ok. They're back in. You can turn on the power."

There was that hum again and then the elevator slowly started up. To my surprise, it passed the thirty-ninth floor, and then I remembered that Marie had asked for the forty-seventh. Sure enough, the door opened there and I was so relieved I wanted to hug someone.

I was nearest to the door and was about to get out, when the tall guy stepped in front of me and blocked the way. Marie leaned out and looked up and down the hall.

"It's clear Scotty. Come on out."

The wheelchair rolled through the door and still the tall man stood in front of me. His hand was on the hold button. Then he pulled a gun from under his jacket.

"Don't get out, lady," he said. "Go up to your floor, get out and wait there."

He pushed me back deeper into the elevator, took his hand off the hold button and stepped out. The door closed. The elevator started up and I was all alone. I had no idea what was going on.

I almost panicked again, but already the door was opening on the forty-ninth and believe me I raced out of there.

A cop was standing in the hallway.

"Lady," he said, "you're very lucky."

"How did you know about it?" I asked. What the hell was going on?

"The wheelchair guy and the lady pushing him robbed a bank about an hour ago. Somebody got their get-away plates and saw her putting on the wig. Car was stolen but since we knew the plates we could track them with GPS.

"Why didn't they arrest them?" I was thinking how much aggravation it would have saved me.

"Too many people on the street to do anything right then. They turned into this parking garage and she pulled the wheelchair out of the back of the car and he got in it. They must have stashed it there before the robbery. We could see them, but a truck blocked the entrance and we just missed grabbing them. They must have taken the freight elevator up to the lobby. By the way, the big guy, the one with the briefcase, is a Fed, a Federal Agent.

My mind was reeling. So that's why he'd been so out of breath. That's why he had a gun. Everything was falling into place.

"Where were they going?" I asked.

"Don't know that yet for sure. We'll find out soon enough. There were enough cops on the forty-seventh to catch a regiment. They won't get away. Incidentally, there wasn't anything wrong with the elevator. We just stopped it so we could buy time to get some more cops here. We were sorry to put you in harm's way, but there wasn't anything we could do about it. We figured at least the Fed guy was there. Anyway, like I said, you're a lucky lady. We'll need a statement from you, of course, and your ID, but then you can be on your way.

Well, they did catch Scotty and Marie, but oddly enough I felt sort of sorry for them. They seemed so inept, so pathetic somehow.

The story was all over the TV and the newspapers, of course, because of the size of the bank robbery and how fast the cops caught the robbers. They got some things wrong, like saying I had been a hostage, but I did get my picture on TV and the papers and I had lots of calls. Thinking about it afterwards though I realized that none of that would have happened to me if I hadn't had a run in my pantyhose.

NEIGHBORS

I was still in my nightgown when the doorbell rang. "It's your neighbor, Carole, from across the street," came a voice through the door. "I need to use your phone."

Carole? My neighbor? Oh yes, I remembered, the fleshy, blowzy-looking blonde in her forties, with the red-painted Dragon Lady fingernails, the only renter on the block. She'd been living there for a little over a year, but we'd hardly exchanged a dozen words beyond, "Hi. How are you?" in all that time.

She wore expensive-looking, but trendy clothes and flashy jewelry, and she wobbled around in four inch heels, looking like she'd topple over any minute. I guess it was uncharitable of me, but when she wore those tight black leather pants tucked into high black boots, I couldn't help thinking of a sausage stuffed into its casing. Mostly I just saw her easing in and out of a scarlet BMW.

I knew from another neighbor that Carole had been feuding with the owner of the house, and I'd recently seen a small U-Haul parked in front, being loaded with some possessions, but it wasn't until the banner went up that I realized there was a Hatfield and McCoy situation going on over there.

The banner read: "Attention owner Johnson: Not responsible for any damage to this house." It was signed, "C. Thomas." Someone had tacked it across the fascia board in front of the house. I didn't know the details, but my next-door neighbor, Anne, told me Carole was in arrears in her lease payments and the owner had given her notice to vacate.

When I opened the door, Carole asked permission to use my phone. She said that the owner had put new locks on the door and locked her out. She was furious that she couldn't get into the house and wanted to call her lawyer.

It was an awkward situation and I tried to make myself scarce and give her some privacy, but I live in a very open house and couldn't help overhearing Carole's side of the conversation.

She explained to the lawyer about the locks and said she'd arranged for a furniture van to be over at twelve o'clock. "I need to pack stuff. The movers need to get in." Her voice had become high-pitched and whiny, and she seemed to be about to cry.

"October fifteenth? You mean I have two more weeks? I wish you'd told me that before. I've been living with a friend in Balboa. So what do I do about the locks?"

There was a long pause while she listened. "That's legal? You're sure?" Her tone was disbelieving and relieved at the same time.

When she got off the phone, she was smiling. "He says to get a locksmith out and have him open the door, that I have another two weeks to go from the notice-to-move date."

I tried to look puzzled. I didn't want her to know the neighbors had been gossiping about her.

"I guess you don't know the Johnsons gave me an eviction notice." She sounded righteous and angry. "They claim I owe them five thousand dollars, but it's only three thousand. They say I caused damage to their hardwood floors, but it's not my fault the refrigerator leaked. I lost my job, and I didn't have the money to fix it and…"

Her voice trailed off. Then her tone changed to indignation. "Someone followed my car yesterday. I saw them in the mirror. I stopped at a supermarket, and when I came out, all four of my tires were slashed. I called the police, and they came out and said yes, the tires were cut deliberately, but there were no witnesses, and I should just call my insurance company."

My curiosity was peaked. "But who would do that? And why? What does it have to do with the house?"

"Spite," she said, "They're trying to get even with me. Well, I've got to call the locksmith. Have you got a yellow pages?"

When I handed her the book, she didn't thank me, and she made several calls to locksmiths before she found one who could come out right away, but she never asked if it was all right to use the phone again.

"Is it ok for me to wait here awhile? He said he'd be over in twenty minutes."

"Sure," I said, and then the phone rang. It was a friend of mine who said she'd just realized she'd left a pot boiling on the stove, and would I use my key to go in and turn the stove off?

I threw a long coat over my nightgown, left Carole in the house, and drove to my friend's. When I returned, Carole was just getting ready to leave, and the locksmith had arrived. Later I saw workmen loading the moving van, so I guessed the locksmith had let her in.

A few days later, as I was gardening our front, the owner of the house pulled up in her Jaguar. She's another blonde, but slim and elegant, with a penchant for couturier clothes that whisper "expensive". She wore beige linen slacks, a white silk blouse and a diamond ring the size of a walnut. I knew her name was Janice, and my neighbor, Anne, said that Janice's first husband had died, and she'd inherited a lot of money. Basically, Anne said, it was Janice who'd poured money into remodeling the house four years ago, when she'd first moved in with her second husband. After about three years, through, she'd decided they needed a three car garage, and went searching for another house. They'd spent a bundle remodeling the second house, too, before they moved in. I knew that, because they happened to buy next door to a friend of mine.

Anyway, Janice dusted off the car trunk, and sat down on it. Then she beckoned me over and pointed to a workman, who was doing something near her front door.

"You know what that SOB, Carole, did?" she asked me. "Broke the new locks I put on the door. Spite! Pure spite! Now that guy over there has to fix it. She owes me five thousand bucks in back rent, besides all the damage she did. We're going to have to refinish the floors, and she ruined the carpeted area, too. And my husband lost his job three months ago." She took a deep breath. "Now we'll have two houses to carry. Know what I found out? She owned a condo, and even though she'd borrowed forty thousand dollars from her mother the condo went into repo."

The breezy contractions reminded me that Janice was a real estate agent. Now she was really warming to her subject. "So what does she do? She has tenants, a little old couple, and she tells them to move, though she doesn't say why. But they want to stay, so she says OK, if they pay her a year's rent in advance! And they did, and she took it, and she didn't even own it anymore! I tell you, she's a crook!" That speech was more than she'd said to me in the whole time she lived across the street.

"What are you going to do?" I asked.

"Sue her, of course, but what good will it do? I found out she doesn't even own that flashy car." Inadvertently, I glanced at the Jag, but Janice didn't seem to notice. "So, we can't even attach that. I'll try to sell the house, but the market's pretty slow right now. I not making much any more."

The workman was finished, and she went over to pay him, and I went back into my house.

Within the week, a For Sale sign went up, and for a couple of months, there was an open house every Sunday. Then a For Rent sign appeared, and after a few weeks, the sign came down, and I saw a moving truck in front of the house. There's a new neighbor now, a fortyish woman, who's in the process of getting a divorce, according to Anne, who seems to know everything that's going on in the neighborhood. There's a friendly teenage boy who says they're leasing for a year, and a pretty teenage girl who smokes a lot.

My cleaning lady used to work for Carole, the first renter. She says Carole lost her job because she talked back to the boss, and that's why she's broke. But she also says Carole's a con artist who bled her mother white. She tells me that after Carole vacated the house, she moved in with a a sleazy boyfriend, fought with him, and moved out again. It seems that

Carole calls her from time to time, and cries on her shoulder.

The funny thing about all this is that I hardly knew either Janice, the owner, or Carole, the renter, until all this started. Now I feel as though I could write a novel about them, if my cleaning lady ever tells me the end of the story.

What bothers me, though, is that I left Carole alone in the house for at least twenty minutes, when I checked on that pot on my friend's stove. Given Carole's track record, I guess I was lucky that nothing disappeared while I was gone.

MISSIONARIES

I ain't never been to nothin' like it before, but I seen this here show advertised in the newspapers, and I guess I was curious about it. It was a bunch of photos from the 1930's by WPA photographers. I grew up during the depression, you see, and I remember this lady and her big old camera comin' 'round… but I'm gettin' ahead of my story.

Anyways, I went 'round the corner of this here museum into the second room, and there was this one picture that almost jumped off the wall at me. I felt like I imagine people do when they take a stiff drink on a empty stomach. See, I never 'spected to see it again, let alone in any museum.

I don't think it would have hit anybody else like that… only my pa, and he's long gone. The picture is pretty ordinary, I guess. It just shows an old fishin' boat, little cabin in front, and an old oil barrel on deck, but painted all over the cabin are these slogans:

129

"ONLY JESUS SAVES"
"BIBLES"
"MARANATHA (THE LORD COMETH)"

and that last, the Maranatha, that was the name of the boat, too. But out on deck are these two people, a man, maybe forty or so, and a boy 'bout sixteen, both of them in old work clothes. Underneath the picture it say, "Missionaries on the Mississippi".

The thing is, the man in that picture is my pa, way younger'n I am now, and the boy, well, that's me. We're standin' with our hands behind our backs and just sort of lookin' at the camera, real serious-like.

All these old mem'ries started comin' back at me. I 'membered that lady with the funny big camera takin' the picture, I didn't know why, and people sayin' that President Roosevelt, he was just makin' jobs for them photographers and the people who painted pictures on the walls, just like he did for the fellas that was workin' on the roads, or in the forests.

Lookin' at the picture, I began rememberin' why Pa started that missionary boat in the first place, and

how it changed my whole life. See, Pa was a fisher-
man, only during the depression, not too many people had money to buy the fish he caught, and even
when they did, they didn't pay much for them. Well,
we was eatin' fish and nothing else for the third day
runnin' when Pa saw this poster about this revival
lady and how she was holdin' a big meetin' in a tent
out at the fairgrounds.

Make a long story short, Pa went to the meetin',
me in tow, and when the collection plate went round,
and he saw all that money in it, I thought his eyes
would pop right out of his head. It wasn't that people
could give that much, but when you put all those offerin's together, it was a pretty tidy amount… more
than Pa made in a couple of weeks fishin'.

He was quiet all the next day, but once he decided, there was no stoppin' him. He'd made up his
mind to go into the missionary business, and nobody
could've talked him out of it. 'Course, he couldn't afford a great big tent like the lady had, but Pa had a
idea. He got ahold of some white paint, and painted
the whole cabin of the boat white. Then he got some
black paint, too, and painted them slogans on it. He
bought some Bibles, too, and made some wooden

benches and some posters. Then he sailed that fishin' boat three or four towns down the Mississippi, docked the boat and put the posters announcin' a revival meetin' out on the dock and all 'round the town.

Maybe a dozen people showed up, more for somethin' to do than 'cause they was religious, you see. Now Pa, he was a religious man, but he didn't have the gift. Wasn't nobody screamin' and hollerin' in tongues when he preached, and he didn't sell but one Bible, nor collect much in the offerin' plate neither.

We tried three or four towns in the next week, but it was plain it wasn't goin' to work. Pa, he got kind of quiet for a while, and then he said to me, "Son, you give it a try. Maybe you're better at preachin' than I am."

Truth is, it was the last thing I wanted to do, but Pa was bound and determined, so in the next town, with a shove from Pa, I stood up and commenced talkin'. Trouble was, I wasn't any better at it than Pa was and for a fact we didn't sell even one Bible, or take in more'n a few cents. Me, I was ready to give it up for sure, but Pa said we had to at least sell the rest of them Bibles.

Anyways, we sailed down another town or two, and set up the benches again. Pa give me a shove, and there I was, out in front of maybe a couple dozen people, wonderin' what to say. I looked up, and there was this real pretty gal, sittin' right up in the front row. Lookin' at her, I could feel somethin' stirrin' inside of me. I don't know what got into me, but the spirit of the Lord just took over. The next thing I knowed, there was this big fat lady rollin' 'round on the floor and makin' these funny noises. Pretty soon, a couple o' more people joined in, yellin' and dancin', and I couldn't stop preachin'.

Well, we must've sold eight Bibles that day, and there was a pretty nice take in the offerin' plate, and Pa said that was that, I was goin' to be the preacher in the family.

In the next town we stopped at, I looked 'round till I saw a pretty gal and waited for the Lord to put his hand on me again, and sure enough I got that same stirrin', and the words started pourin' out of me, and the people was speakin' in tongues and tearin' at their clothes. Then this one lady come up to me in a wheelchair and said she couldn't walk and would I lay my hands on her and pray. I started to say I

133

couldn't do that, but she grabbed my hand and put it in her lap, so I just started prayin' and prayin' and darned if that lady didn't up and walk.

Well, we sold all the Bibles we had, and could've sold more and Pa's eyes got sort of misty when he saw that collection plate. Another town and another, and the same thing happened, the crowds getting a little bit bigger each time as word o' mouth got round, and I guess that's how it would have stayed 'cept that in this one town, Majorie showed up.

Majorie, she's the preacher lady that had the big tent and all, that first gave Pa his idea. She said I had the gift, more'n she did, but she had what she called the knowhow, and if Pa and I would let her be our manager and do our publicity for us, she could put us in the big time, like Billy Sunday or Amy McPherson. Pa thought about that for a bit and after a while, he agreed.

Time we got to the next town, Majorie had it plastered all over with these here posters, announcin' about our faith-healin' in her big tent, and there was maybe a couple hundred people from towns all 'round waitin' to hear us. It took both Pa and Majorie to pass around the plate and sell the Bibles.

We started havin' these revivals every week or so, travelin' up and down the Mississippi, and the money was comin' in like you wouldn't believe. After a while, maybe a year or two, Majorie bought this big shiny Cadillac, and Pa bought a great big old house down in Biloxi that was built 'fore the War Between the States, and had a lawn as big as a football field that sloped right down to the water.

I got to thinkin' 'bout it and my conscience started botherin' me. I went to Pa and Majorie and I told them how I felt, and didn't Jesus say to give everything away to the poor and all. Well, they listened a while, and then Majorie said we was doin' the Lord's work, and the Lord wouldn't want us to be hungry or uncomfortable, or we wouldn't be able to do a good job for Him, and Pa said we was just bein' a example of how the Lord rewards people who spread his word, and I could see how maybe that was right.

Well, I guess you know the rest. After a while, Pa and Majorie got married, and 'bout five years later, I got married, too, to one o' them pretty gals from in the audience. Majorie and her got to be great pals, and they was always shoppin' together and everything. Pa and Majorie, and then Cindy… she's my wife... they all took over the business end of things so's I could concentrate on the preachin'. Then, after Pa died, Majorie and Cindy took care of it all by theirselves. So, here I am now with this big television station, and a Bible school named after me and all that.

The thing is, I never planned on being no preacher, but Pa said you couldn't disagree with success, and the Lord's ways was mysterious. 'Course I know that's true, but sometimes I can't help wonderin' what would've happened to my life if Pa had been better at preachin' than he was, or if that pretty little gal hadn't showed up at that second meetin', or if Majorie hadn't come along when she did.

One thing for sure. I wouldn't't've been wearin' this five hundred dollar suit, or these two-hundred-fifty dollar shoes, and I wouldn't be here in New York City, lookin' at these old photos. Pa's right, you know. The Lord's ways surely is mysterious.

TERROR

Alice comes awake, drowsily, to the sensation of something tickling her left arm. Still half asleep, she is about to brush at it, when suddenly the source of the tickle comes into focus.

The hair on the back of her neck stiffens. A cold sweat soaks her nightgown. Goosebumps break out all over her skin. The shiny creature on her arm is a black widow spider. She is terrified that it will bite.

The phone rings. It is her wake-up call, she knows,, but she is afraid to pick it up. It rings seven times, eight, but she cannot move to answer it. She envisions the spider biting her, imagines herself dying slowly, agonizingly, as the phone continues to ring.

The spider walks along her arm, in a slow, dignified stroll. It pays no attention to the incessant ringing. It is aiming for something above her head. Alice shifts her eyes upward, while the rest of head and body remain frozen.

Peripherally, her eyes catch silver strands, defined by a sunbeam that streams through an errant gap in the blinds. They lead from the lamp to the wall behind the bed, a perfect and empty web. The spider carries nothing, no victim fly or moth, alive and paralyzed, to bind with silken threads within the web.

The phone, probably automated, will not stop ringing. Alice begins to wonder if she is losing her mind, or is trapped in a Kofkaesque nightmare. The spider pauses at the first shining strand, but makes no move to climb onto it.

One minute. Two. It sits on her shoulder. Something in Alice snaps. An unearthly shriek reverberates from the walls. With one accurate blow, she smashes the spider against her shoulder. The phone stops ringing.

ROSES AND THE BAG LADY

Since I go out for my coffee break at the same time every morning, I couldn't help noticing the older woman who repeatedly stood on that busy Wilshire corner. She and a leashed, mangy dog have been there every day for a week, but today she has the dog in a shopping cart that also contains a battered old valise and what looks like a box of long-stemmed roses.

It occurred to me that if my birth mother was still alive, she would be about the same age as the woman. I couldn't help wondering if my mother, too, had fallen on hard times.

I didn't know anything at all about my birth mother. The people who had adopted me were very good and kind, and I loved them dearly, but they had never talked about my real mother, and when I was older and asked them directly, they said it was better to let sleeping dogs lie. That only made me more curious about the circumstances of my birth.

I'd been intending for some time to hire a detective to see if he could track my mother down, but somehow I didn't do it. Maybe I was afraid of what I would find, or that I'd be rejected. I don't know. I just know I hadn't done it.

Now here was this bag lady, and, of course, the idea, what if she was my mother, crossed my mind, but I knew it was too far fetched. Still, for the sake of that unknown parent, I decided to approach the woman and see if she needed help.

"Excuse me." I said to her. "You appear to be lost. Can I help you?"

"Oh no dearie. I'm not lost. I'm out here to sell these roses. You want to buy one?" She flashed me a gap-toothed smile. "They're only two dollars apiece. It's so me and the dog can eat, you see. Scotty's got something wrong with his leg, too, and we need to see a vet. That's why I put him in the cart, so's he won't hurt it any more."

I took my wallet out of my purse and handed her the money for a single rose. I tried to refuse the flower, thinking she could sell it again, but she insisted that I take it. "I'm not pan-handling," she told me proudly. "I'm just trying to make a living."

She open the valise, which, it turned out, she was using as a bank or cash register of sorts, and put the two dollars inside. I caught a glimpse of a small pile of bills before she snapped the lid. It seemed to me that she'd be an easy mark for any predator who saw her put the money there, and I said something to that effect, but she just smiled. "Been through a lot in my life. I'm a tough old bird. I can take care of myself, and anyway, I have the dog to protect me."

Looking at the scruffy creature, I couldn't imagine him protecting anyone except, perhaps, by giving the attacker rabies, but I let it pass, and went back to my office. I couldn't get the woman out of my mind though and kept wondering about what had happened to my own birth mother. That evening I began looking through the telephone directory for a detective agency, one that specialized in finding people, if there was such a thing.

To my surprise, I found several. One ad in particular appealed to me, and I called the next day. I was startled when a woman answered. I don't know why… maybe all those detective programs on television… but I expected a man. She sounded cordial enough as she listed her fees and what she would try to do. Then to my surprise, she said, "You might not need me at all. If you know your birth name, or your mother's, or what hospital you were born in, there are agencies that might be able to help you for just the expenses they incur."

Unfortunately, I knew none of those things, but it did increase my confidence in Alice Conners as she was called. I felt she wouldn't be just out to gouge me, so I made an appointment for the very next day after work. I had anticipated a young woman, because the voice on the phone was so spritely, but Alice turned out to be about the same age as the bag lady whose pathetic appearance had somehow finally pushed me into pursuing my search.

Unlike the woman on the street corner, however, the detective was smartly dressed in a dark suit and ruffled blouse, and she wore her hair in a short grey bob. I was nervous, and to ease my tension, I asked, "How did you happen to get into this business?"

A shadow crossed her face. "Funny, nobody ever asked me that before. But it's a long story. I think we'd better get on with whatever you can tell me."

There wasn't much I could tell her though. The birth certificate I had seen was only a copy, and it had been altered by my adoptive parents to substitute their names. Maybe they were afraid I'd go looking for my birth mother and they would lose me. I don't know. But they had obliterated the name of the hospital as well. I did know the city, though. I was born in New York. I was certain of that. The city seal was on the certificate.

The only thing I could tell Alice was my date of birth. That had not been erased. September 14, 1956, the document said, so I know I am forty-one.

When I looked up, Alice had turned pale. "You asked me before how I got into this business. I had a daughter once that I gave up for adoption. My husband had died in an automobile accident two months before the baby was born. We had decided to mortgage everything a short time before that so he could start a new business. He was an engineer and an inventor and we had high hopes for its success. But when he died I was left with crushing debts, and there was no way I could take care of the baby. It broke my heart, but I gave her up for adoption. I had to agree not to be told the names of the adoptive parents, or where they lived.

"As soon as I could afford it, I began to search for my daughter, but I kept hitting up against a brick wall. No names, no addresses. Meanwhile, though, I'd learned so much about how to research information that I decided to go into this business. The thing is…" She paused and her voice quavered. "The thing is that my daughter was born in New York City on September 14, 1956."

My heart leaped. Was it possible? I wanted to believe it with all my being and I knew Alice did too. Because we both gave consent, the hospital, which, of course, Alice knew, released a fax of the original birth certificate. There was no doubt about it, by the craziest chance, I had found my real mother.

We hugged and kissed and cried. We sat and talked for hours, but naturally I had to go back to work the next day. When I went out for my coffee break, there was the bag lady, still with the valise and the mangy dog, and red roses in the shopping cart.

I rushed up to her. "You won't understand," I told her, "but you did something wonderful for me, and I want to pay for Scotty's trip to the vet." I handed her a hundred dollar bill. "And I want to buy all the roses you have," I said smiling. "They're for my mother."

A MARRIAGE MADE IN HEAVEN

From all the way across the parking lot I can see Ethel waving the paper and my heart sinks. The last thing I want to do is drive all the way out to Palm Springs and back, but I only recently remarried and I don't want to get off on the wrong foot with my new husband's elderly sister, who's visiting us from back east.

As she approaches, sparkles of excitement bubble out of her, like seltzer from a glass.

"I found it! I found the address! I thought the paper was lost and then when I was under the hair dryer, I found it all scrunched up in a corner of my purse."

She's short and plump and the flesh above her bra and her freshly bleached blond curls bobble in unison in her enthusiasm.

Well, I guess there's no help for it, we'll have to go. Ethel's been talking about her dear old friend, Betty, for two days now.

"Imagine, she was a widow for ten years, just like me" Ethel confided. "Her first husband, Bernie, a nice man (may he rest in peace) left her plenty of money. But being a widow is lonely."

Ethel sighs and pauses. "Who should know that better than me?"

Then about a year ago, according to Ethel, Jack, who used to play cards with Betty's late husband, sought Betty out after his late wife's death. He courted and won her. Those were the words she used, courted and won. It sounded to me like a Victorian romance novel.

"Such a wonderful gentleman!" Ethel enthuses. "How lucky Betty is. It's a marriage made in heaven!" She used that phrase repeatedly, from the time she first proposed that we visit her friend.

So, now, with the crumpled paper in hand, she makes the arrangements by phone, as soon as we get back from the beauty parlor and by ten the next morning we're out on the Freeway. Ethel had been up and twittering in front of the mirror since six. She'd changed her dress and fussed with her hair again so many times that I'd begun to wonder if we'd ever get started.

While we're driving, she tells me that she'd spoken to, but not seen Betty, since twelve years ago, when Betty's late husband (may he rest in peace) I mouth silently along with her, was still alive.

I do a double take. "Then how do you know so much about this new guy, what's his name… Jack? I thought you'd met him."

"No," Ethel concedes, she hasn't. But Betty has told her. That phrase pops out again. "It's a marriage made in heaven, absolutely."

When we finally get there, Betty turns out to look pretty much the way I'd expected. She's small and plump, like Ethel, with large brown eyes and delicate features. She's in her seventies, with the inevitable pile-up of bleached blond hair, vivacious, friendly, warm and rather earthy.

Gentleman Jack, on the other hand, is somewhat of a surprise. He's about two inches shorter than Betty, seventy-five-ish, dapper and trim, with a crest of marceled white hair, a neat mustache, gold-rimmed glasses and a very courtly manner.

He insists on taking all of us ladies out to lunch. In the driveway, Betty climbs into the driver's seat and Jack sits beside her. Ethel and I slide into the back.

"You're driving, Betty?" Ethel sounds incredulous. "You never drove when Bernie (may he rest in peace) was alive. You always hated driving."

"It's only a short distance," Betty says rather defensively. "Jack has these cataracts and it's hard for him to drive."

White-knuckled, we negotiate the six blocks to Palm Drive in silence and screech into the restaurant's parking space. I make a mental note to offer to drive on the way back.

As we wait for our table, Jack is very sweet to Ethel and me and attentive to his wife. He urges all of us to try the lobster, or the rack of lamb, which turn out to be the most expensive things on the menu. When the maitre d' shows us to our booth, Jack squeezes in next to me, but I seem to be the only one who thinks that's a bit odd.

I find it stranger still, when, during the soup course, his left hand starts to fondle my knee under the table, even as his right hand is raised in a toast to "My beautiful wife". Still, Betty and Ethel are so happy, I decide not to make an issue of it and just quietly remove the offending paw. Jack's smile never changes.

Back at the house, we sit on the terrace soaking up sun. Jack is every inch the gracious host and husband. He sets up extra chairs, brings drinks and continues to charm Ethel and his wife.

At a pause in the conversation, Ethel turns to Jack and asks, "What did you do before you retired?"

"Oh, Jack didn't exactly retire," Betty answers for him. "He was in the jewelry business. His partner… it was something to do with the books. I don't understand it all. Anyway, the business failed about three years ago, but it wasn't Jack's fault. You explain it, Jack."

"Now Betty, I'm not going to bore the ladies with that old stuff. I'm retired. Enough!" There's a testy edge to his voice, but he's still smiling. "Come on girls. How about another drink?"

After a bit, I excuse myself to go to the bathroom. Jack slides open the glass patio door for me and to my surprise follows me inside. I think maybe he's going to show me where the bathroom is, but as we round a corner, he quickly opens a closet door and shoves me inside. He slides in after me and closes the door behind him.

"How about a kiss, honey," he says. His arm snakes around my waist, and his hand heads for my butt.

I panic for a second and then instinct prevails. He's such a flyweight, it doesn't take much to shove him out of the way and open the door.

"Listen Jack", I hiss, "I don't want to have to tell your wife and Ethel about this."

That courtly smile never changes. Hurriedly, I duck into the bathroom and lock the door behind me. I stay there for as long as I decently can, thinking all the while, Jesus, what if old Romeo is still out there when I come out. I'd hate to make a scene and spoil it for the ladies.

But Jack has retreated to the balcony and is as unctuous as an undertaker when I come back out. After a reasonable interval, I suggest that Ethel and I ought to be getting back because we have a long drive ahead.

Chirpings and embracing between Betty and Ethel take a few minutes. I sidestep Jack pretty gracefully I think. At last we're on our way, Ethel almost splitting between euphoria and envy, but then her generous nature gets the upper hand.

"What did I tell you? she enthuses. "Such a wonderful gentleman. I'm so happy for Betty. It's a marriage made in heaven."

MARY'S STAND-IN

I'm a licensed clinical social worker. My office is on the ground floor of a psychiatric hospital. I'd seen six clients that day, all with serious issues and I was tired. I'd have loved to go home and relax in a tub, but my daughter has the lead in a play her class is presenting that night. Of course, I'd have gone anyway, but since she is an eight year old, when she left in the morning, she'd grabbed the bag with her costume, but forgotten the most important part of it, her crown.

She's a serious and artistic kid and had asked me the day before to take her to a craft shop because she didn't want to just use a yellow crayon on the crown. She wanted gold foil and some "jewels" so it would look, as she said, "real". She worked long and hard covering the cardboard with the foil, smoothing it so there would be no wrinkles, then adhering the "jewels". Actually it would have passed muster even in an adult play.

She'd set is aside to dry at night on top of the washing machine, but in a hurry to leave in the morning, she'd forgotten the crown was not in the bag. When she realized she didn't have it, she called me on my cell phone and I promised I'd come to the school early with it.

I was just putting on my coat when the intercom crackled.

"ATTENTION! ATTENTION! LOCK YOUR DOORS! A PATIENT HAS ESCAPED FROM THE LOCKED WARD ON FOUR. HE IS DELUSIONAL AND HAS A KNIFE. HE IS WANDERING THE HALLS. SECURITY IS LOOKING FOR HIM, BUT THEY HAVEN'T FOUND HIM YET. AGAIN, LOCK YOUR DOORS."

Damn it, I thought. I'll probably be stuck here for hours while they do lockdown. I'll be very late for the play and Alice won't have her crown. She's going to be very upset. I'll call her, but I don't want to explain and scare her. The patient is probably still up on four, but I'd better go lock my door, just in case.

I was just about to do it when a man pushed it open and burst in. He looked wild-eyed and was brandishing a large knife.

"You killed Jesus!" He shouted. "Mary says I have to kill you because of what you did."

THINK, I told myself! Your life depends on it!

I was shaking inside, but as calmly as I could I said, "I'm the real Mary and you're making a terrible mistake. If you kill me, Jesus will never forgive you for killing his mother."

Suddenly I remembered the crown and pulled it from the bag.

"Look at my crown," I said. "Jesus gave it to me so you'd know I was his real mother. That woman who says she's Mary is lying to you. She was sent by Satan. You don't want to make that mistake. Jesus would be very upset with you. Get down on your knees and give me the knife. Ask Jesus to forgive you."

He stared at the crown for a long minute and then deflated like a ballon without air. He got down on his knees and handed me the knife.

"Mary," he said, "forgive me. I didn't know you were the real Mary. But Jesus wouldn't have given you the crown otherwise."

I slid the knife into the bag out of his reach and taking him by the hand, I said, "I forgive you," and led him gently to the door. I pressed the intercom button and said in a calm voice. "There's a man here who's lost. He was looking for Mary, but it's OK now. He needs help getting home."

By the time I opened the door security was there and the patient went with them, calm as a lamb. A different security office confiscated the knife. I didn't mention the crown. I was afraid they might confiscate that, too.

I had to fill out a statement and of course that took time.

Then I phoned my daughter. "I'll be a little late," I said, "I'll explain later. See if you can stall a little longer."

POWER FAILURE

At 8:15 on a cloudy spring morning, Maryanne Martin sits across from the door at the back end of the fourth car of the IRT local heading into Manhattan. She's on her way to work as a file clerk in a lawyer's office, a job she detests.

A moment before, the car had been crowded with other hapless souls on their way to work, but at Atlantic Avenue in Brooklyn, most of them had opted to cross over to the express train on the other side of the platform and now the car is relatively empty.

Maryanne, who's in her late twenties, eyes the remaining passengers with a mixture of suspicion and curiosity. At the front end of the car stand two teenage white boys with shaved heads, tattoos and black clothing. She notes the taller of the two even has a tattoo across his forehead. It appears to be writing of some sort, but she can't make it out at this distance.

As she watches the boys sway with the train's movements, their expressions, Maryanne thinks, are solemn and grim, not what one usually expects from teenagers. Her mind registers possible danger. She regrets that she didn't change at Atlantic, but she had wanted a seat and the express was always crowded at this hour.

Across from the white boys, in the middle of the front end of the car are seated to rather tall black males, whom Maryanne takes to be about the same age as the white boys. They're wearing oversized shirts and baggy pants, which drag on the floor. They're laughing and talking loudly.

More potential trouble. Maryanne worries, especially if there's any kind of verbal exchange between the two groups. Like most New York subway riders she's learned to be alert for signs of danger. She toys with the idea of moving up a few cars when the train stops.

At the moment things are quiet and she turns her attention to the people opposite her in the back section of the car. Directly across from her are two middle-aged white women, dressed for the city. Playing the game she usually does to pass the time on the subway, Maryanne decides that they are probably on their way to shop and maybe see a matinee in Manhattan. No problem there. She studies their clothing and jewelry, envious of people who don't have to go to boring jobs.

On Maryanne's side of the car, sharing the long bench with her is a take-charge looking man. She notes his highly polished shoes, dark suit and red tie. She guesses he is a businessman, on his way to the office. He appears to be in his early fifties and she wonders whether he'd be any help if the teenagers started something.

Finally, in the corner, at the far end, on the side opposite her, sit two women, small and olive-skinned. Their coats are worn and shabby and their shoes are run-over, but there's a flamboyant note in the brightly colored dresses that peak from beneath their coats.

Continuing her game, Maryanne decides that they are Mexican cleaning women, on their way to jobs cleaning houses for women like the ones opposite her, the ones she envies. They talk in Spanish and giggle quietly.

She notches her tension down a bit. No threat on this side of the car she tells herself, but she eyes the two white boys and the two black ones again, still worrying that there is the potential for a fight that could spill over.

She's been longing for some excitement in her life, but not that kind. She's been riding the train five days a week into Manhattan in the morning and back to Brooklyn at night. Her job is dull and her life is going nowhere. She's not married and nobody's on the horizon. She considers herself plain, though people often remark that her eyes are pretty and she knows that she does have beautiful hair. Last week her stylist told her it was good enough to be on a TV commercial.

Leaning back in her seat, she unfolds her newspaper. Andy Warhol said everyone would have their fifteen minutes of fame, she tells herself, but I think he's wrong about me. I don't think my name will ever be in the paper. My life is too uninteresting. She scans the screaming headline on the Daily News and is about to turn the page, when abruptly, the train jerks to a stop and the lights go out.

She's not particularly alarmed at first, for this happens in the tunnel from time to time, but as the moments stretch on and the train remains dark and halted, she worries the the teen-agers may take advantage of the situation. Before she can flesh out the scenario in her mind, the smell of smoke drifts into the car.

There is no announcement of an emergency. Does the PA system require electricity, she wonders. Is the electricity off completely? Is that why the train doesn't move and the lights still don't come on?

The smoke is getting thicker. Suddenly she thinks about the doors. If there is an emergency and the power is off, will the doors open? She is about to stand up and grope her way to the nearest door in the center of the car, when, from the front end, she hears a voice, Southern accented, say loudly, "Looks like we got trouble, people. Don't nobody stand up. Slide along your seat in the direction of the door till you reach the end or bump into somebody. If you do, take their hand, but don't stand up, 'cause we gonna try to open the fuckin' doors, so don't crowd in on us."

The smoke is getting denser. The two matinee ladies are sort of whimpering. The Spanish-speaking women are repeating over and over, "Que pasa? Que pasa?" The begin to pray aloud, "Ayudanos, Jesus. Ayudanos."

Another voice from the front shouts something in rapid-fire Spanish, and she hears the two Mexican women sliding along the seat.

Maryanne feels a sweaty palm seek out her hand. It's the business type, the one she'd hoped might take charge in an emergency. He's whispering to himself, "Somebody, somebody, help." He sounds a bit unhinged.

There's a commotion at the door. An unaccented voice is cursing loudly.

"Get your hand in front of the rubber strip on the door and push when I count three," the voice says. "It's the only way we're gonna move this mother-fucking door. Ready now, one, two, three. Push!"

Maryanne hears grunts and more cursing, but there is no sound of an opening door. The smoke is thick. Everyone's coughing. Maryanne can feel her eyes smarting and tearing. She's beginning to panic.

"Everybody get down on the floor. There's less smoke there," says the southern accent, "but don't crawl over here till we get the door open."

There is the sound of bodies moving as they obey. The businessman is repeating like a mantra, "Please, God please God, please."

"Quick," the voice at the door demands. "We need to work together. You, white guys, put your hands on the strip, too. Wait for the count of three and push."

In the dark, Maryanne hears bodies positioning themselves at the door, and then, after the count, loud grunting. Gratefully she hears the doors slide back.

"Ok, now we're going out by the numbers," the same voice says. "I stuck my foot out of the car. There's a four foot drop between the car and the walkway, so you on the door side, let yourself down and then climb up. The walkway is narrow, so hug the wall when you get there and stand up," commands the southern accent.

The order is repeated in Spanish.

"Now you, on the far side, crawl over to the door. Just go across till you feel my feet and then jump down and climb up on the walkway." His voice is hoarse. He coughs repeatedly.

"Hurry," he says.

Maryanne and the businessman are the last to leave. The Southern voice yells, "Yo, anybody still in there?"

Nobody answers, and now they're all out in the tunnel in the pitch dark, choking on the smoke. Maryanne marvels at the way the teenagers are taking charge. It's almost as if they've been trained for an emergency.

"If you have hankies, tie them around your nose and mouth. Then hold hands," The voice that Maryanne thinks is coming from one of the shaved head types says, "Flatten your back against the wall. We're gonna move together along the tunnel till we get to an emergency door. Hold hands. Don't let go."

The line starts to move sideways and forward. They begin to hear hysterical voices and choking and coughing, as people fight their way out of other cars. Maryanne feels the press of bodies milling around. The heat and smoke are stifling.

Again, the Southern voice takes charge, repeating the instructions to the new groups, who obey like children. Order is restored. Hands are joined. The line moves forward.

Suddenly, perhaps two hundred feet ahead, Maryanne can see a faint green light through the smoke.

"Stay together," shouts the shaved head voice. "I'm gonna let go and move up ahead and see if that light is an emergency door. Keep moving!"

Rapid footsteps fade away.

"Dear God, let it be a door!" Maryanne prays.

There's a shout up ahead. "Right on!" The voice exclaims. "It's an emergency door! There are steps to the street. Stay in line. Don't bunch. Don't push. We're all going to get out."

The line inches forward and one by one, people emerge from the tunnel, coughing, choking, eyes streaming.

Maryanne moves with the others, grateful to the two groups of teenagers. The white kids with the shaved heads and the black kids, they saved us all, she thinks.

As they emerge, blinking, into the sunlight, there are emergency vehicles all over the street. They are assaulted by a barrage of cameramen and flashing lights. The reporters overwhelm them with questions: Were they frightened in the tunnel? Is anyone hurt? Did the fire reach their car?

Maryanne is happy just to be treated and allowed to go home.

The next morning, the Daily News has a huge headline:

SUBWAY FIRE
TWO DEAD
COPS CALLED HEROES

43 Treated For Smoke Inhalation
Two elderly women die of smoke inhalation in the first car of a Manhattan-bound train, as fire of suspicious origin engulfs it. The fire causes a power outage and sends thick smoke billowing through the remaining cars and tunnel. Passengers cite undercover cops they'd thought were teenage gang members who led them out of the tunnel. They credit the officers with keeping the crowd disciplined. Everyone cooperated. There was no panic. The potential for greater disaster was averted. Mayor also acclaims two teens who helped.

Puzzled, Maryanne reads the story carefully. What was this about hero cops? What about the teenagers?

She recognizes the black and white guys in the photograph on page one. Their names, occupations and ages are listed underneath. The officers, it turns out, were the black guys in the baggy clothes and they weren't teenagers at all. They'd been assigned to the subway to watch for a man who'd been robbing passengers at gunpoint and sometimes pistol-whipping them. And, of course, the officers had been trained in emergency procedures and crowd control. The white kids had just pitched in to help.

And on page three, is a picture of Maryanne Martin, a file clerk from Brooklyn.

Then the phone begins ringing. An old friend from high school wants to get in touch with her. A boyfriend whom she hasn't heard from in years calls and wants to know if she is all right. He wonders if they can get together for drinks. Another old friend calls and apologizes, says she had no idea where Maryanne lived and wouldn't it be great to get together and talk about old times.

So there's fifteen minutes of fame, for me and the cops and the teenagers, she thinks. Andy Warhol had it right after all.

THE PORNO THEATER

The X-rated movie had not yet begun, but the grimy theater was packed. My date spotted two empty seats off to one side and we immediately stumbled over several knees to get to them.

But there were two sandal-clad, filthy feet propped up on the back of my seat and their owner didn't seem inclined to move them.

My date, Ted, turned and stared at the sandal's owner. "How about getting your feet down and making room for the lady." His voice was sort of threatening.

Mr. Filthy feet crossed his ankles, but otherwise didn't move. "Fuck off and find another seat. I'm comfortable."

I could see the blood rushing to Ted's face. He has a black belt in karate, and I had this sinking feeling that he'd pick up the guy by his feet an turn him into a propeller. I yanked at his sleeve. "Let's move, Ted. Let's not start a fight."

My date ignored me. "One more time, asshole. Move them. Now."

Ted's voice was deadly quiet, but it scared the hell out of me and I thought it would scare the sandal owner too, but all of a sudden the two burly guys on either side of him, guys with faces like gorillas, stood up. "You and what fucking army are going to make him move, huh Tedi-boy?"

With that, Ted grabbed the sandal guy by his legs, lifted him, and tossed him forward, over the seat and into our row. The guy's face smashed down on the seat in front of me and I heard a roar as his two ape buddies started after Ted, their skinheads reflecting the house lights which were now on.

From the back of the theater, the manager and two ushers, who looked like bouncers, came rushing up. They pointed at the skinheads, at Ted and me, and the guy with the filthy feet, who was just coming around.

"Out, all of you," screamed the manager. "Get out now or I'll have you thrown out. I've already called the cops."

The apes had been on the point of wrecking the joint, but when they head the word "cops", they looked at each other and the wind went out of their sails.

Ok, Ok. Cool it. We're going." one of them sputtered, "But throw out them two also. They started it."

The manager pointed at us. "You heard me. Out! I don't care who started it. You're not wrecking my theater." Anybody would have thought he was talking about the Taj Mahal.

I was embarrassed and scared, as Ted and I slunk out of our seats. What would happen when we got out the door and the two gorillas lit into us?

Then I saw the cop at the back and the two bouncers following the skinheads out of the theater and I felt better.

"Wait right there." The cop pointed at the aisle next to the last row of seats. "And don't budge for ten minutes."

All around us people are rubber-necking, yelling and taking sides, but then the house lights went down again, and the panting and pawing on the screen got under way, and they all settled down again.

We waited while the cop went out and checked the street. When he came back, he gave us a thumbs up sign and we left, but I'll tell you one thing. I'm never going to go to an X-rated movie again.

THE LUSH

Stupid driver! Came right at my Caddie, and then he had the nerve to yell at me and give me the finger. I may have had one or two, but I knew what I was doing! Wouldn't 've come out anyway, 'cept that dumb Barry found the bottle I stashed in the hamper under the clothes, and the other bottle in the planter. Dumped 'em both down the sink 'n gave me a lecture 'sif I was a teenager or somethin'. Don't know why I ever married that dumb jerk!

Barry thinks he's a preacher or somethin'. "You've got to stop drinkin" he says, like I was a drunk or somethin'. I'm not a drunk. I just need one or two to get me started is all.

So I came down to this market after ol' Barry left for work. I put a couple of groceries in the basket, and some cheese and crackers, along with some different brands of liquor, so's it'll look like I'm having a party. Don't want any funny looks from the cashier.

Time I got in line, there was this skinny old lady, right in front of me. Same one that stopped me outside the market. Panhandler. Skinny as a mop.

Wanted a couple of dimes, or a quarter. Didn't fool me… probably just gonna lap it up instead of buyin' food. No wonder she's so skinny. Probably doesn't eat at all. Just a boozer.

Her basket's pretty full though. I should 've picked a shorter line. I'm dying for a drink, but now only the one lane is open.

Didn't give the old lady any money outside. Ol' ragbag. Face saggin' like a bulldog. Would've given it to her, but my head hurt and I didn't want to search through my purse for change. Besides, I was in a hurry to get home. Well, not a hurry, 'zactly, I can wait, but I did want to get home.

What's the ol' fleabag doin', anyway? First she had this fistful of coupons she was waving at the clerk, and now she's got food stamps, too. Some people have no consideration.

Move it, lady! My head's splitting. I've got to get home!

Cashier's being nauseatingly sweet to the old lady, considering. Hasn't said a word about the coupons. What's the ol' lady think this is, a welfare state?

Airhead cashier! Big smile for the ol' crone. Lots of stupid chit-chat.

Who does the bird-brain think she's dealin' with, Mother MacCree? Look at the old lady's nails. They're all dirty, and her hair hasn't been combed for a week. Come to think of it, I don't remember combin' mine this morning. Oh well, I just needed that one drink is all. I'll brush my hair when I get home.

Hurry up, lady! What's she doin' now? Oh my God, she's got a sixpack of beer. She can't use food stamps for that. Now there'll be a hassle. Wait. I don't believe it! She's got that paper cup full of nickels and dimes and quarters that she had outside, and she's countin' them out for the beer.

Glad I didn't give her any money, the ol' lush! Come on, ol' lady. Move it! Should be 'shamed of yourself. Hurry up, damn it! I've got to get home. I really need a drink.

TIJUANA INCIDENT

I can't vouch for the authenticity of this story. It was told to me by a casual acquaintance at a cocktail party, who swears that it happened in Tijuana some years ago, before the present reform administration. He insists that he has evidence to prove it.

According to Bob, he, his wife, his sister-in-law, and brother-in-law had gone down to Mexico from Orange County to spend the day. The men were going to go to a Jai-lai game, the women to do some shopping. They planned to meet on Avenida de Revolution, where the man with the zebra-painted donkey takes photos of visitors, both foreign and native. The agreement was that they would meet in three hours.

At the specified time, the women arrived, but the men had not yet appeared. The women waited, taking turns looking into shop windows, but after fifteen minutes they began to get nervous and started pacing back and forth, looking for the men. Several times, a policeman passed by, and after an hour the women, worried about their husbands, were just about to approach him, when he accosted them.

"I am taking you to jail," he told them in English. "I have been watching you for an hour, and you have been loitering on the street, trying to solicit men for purposes of prostitution."

The women protested. They'd been waiting for their husbands, they said.

"For an hour?" was the policeman's skeptical reply. "I do not believe you. Where are these so-called husbands of yours?" Over the women't indignant objections, he carted them off to jail.

There the women were booked, photographed and finger-printed. They were frightened, worried about their husbands, wondering what to do. As they were about to ask for a lawyer, into the station walked their husbands, upset because they couldn't find their wives. The Jai-lai game had started late, they explained, and they had been delayed at the end, making their way through the crowd. When the women were not at the appointed place, the men went to the police.

"Yes," the police confirmed pleasantly, the women were indeed safe; in fact they were here in the jail.

Assuming that the matter was now cleared up, the husbands asked that their wives be released, since it was all a mistake.

"How long will that take?" asked the men. "Oh," the police told them, "probably two or three days. They'll have to stay in jail here until it can be arranged."

The two men were appalled. "Surely there must be some other way to deal with it. You can see that it's a mistake."

The fat sergeant at the desk scratched his scraggly beard and thought for a few minutes. "Well, there is one way."

The men were eager. "What way is that?"

"Well, if you were to buy them licenses to solicit, we could drop the charges."

Their wallets considerably lightened, the four returned to Orange County, but the man who told me the story said that if I wanted to see proof that the story was true, I had only to come to his house, where a framed certificate hangs on the wall, entitling his wife to solicit for purposes of prostitution in the city of Tijuana.

ENCOUNTER IN A CAFE

"Um," this masculine voice says. "Anyone else sitting at this table?"

I look up and see this guy, who would be kind of good looking if he wasn't dressed like such a nerd. He's wearing this red plaid shirt and a cowboy jacket with fringe on the sleeves and a green knit tie! In the middle of Manhattan, for heaven's sake! I wonder if he expects to tie up a horse here. I mean, he has to be a loser!

Anyway, I'm halfway through lunch and it's obvious no one is sitting in the empty place across from me. Still there must be at least ten empty tables in the cafe he could have used.

I shake my head, ungraciously I hope.

"No, nobody."

"Mind if I sit down?" he says.

Well, in fact, I do mind. I mind a lot, but, "It's a free country," I shrug.

Pretty dumb, that, but no dumber than his opener.

He sits down and leans toward me.

"What's good on the menu?" he wants to know.

What am I, psychic, or something? I'm supposed to know what this guy wants to eat? But before I can say anything he's checking out my plate.

"What're you eating?"

Is he blind or what? There are still three shrimp on my plate.

"Looks good," he says. "I think I'll have that too."

Whatever. Suit yourself, fella, I'm thinking. I'll finish my shrimp and I'm gone. You're weird and I'm outta here. I put down some money and start to get up.

"Oh please don't go," he says. "I'm only here on account of you. I followed you. I've been wanting to meet you for a long time. We work in the same building, see, but I couldn't figure out how else to talk to you."

Followed me! He is a weirdo. I feel it in my bones!

"Uh... see," I say. "That's my boyfriend over there. I've been waiting for him. He just came in."

I wave frantically in the general direction of the bar and smile like a Cheshire cat.

Oh, shit. That big hairy gorilla at the bar thinks I'm coming on to him. He's coming over.

"Buy you a drink, little lady?", he says.

Great. Now I've got two of them to deal with!

"Thanks," I say, "but actually I was waving at my boyfriend over there."

I wave toward the bar, look up and hope the floor with open up. There's nobody there but the bartender. I feel like an idiot!

"Well," I tell the nerd. Nice meeting you. I have to go."

He grabs my hand. "Oh, please don't go. Please. Sit down with me. I need to talk to you."

The hairy ape cracks his knuckles. "This guy bothering you?"

How did I get into this? Better yet, how do I get out of it?

"No, no", I say. "It's ok." I sit down again.

"You sure?"

"Yes, yes, it's all right."

The ape gives me a sour look, but goes back to the bar.

"That was really nice of you," says my table mate. "Thanks."

"Look," I say. "Let me be honest. I just didn't want a brawl. I don't know who you are or what you want, but please, please, leave me alone. I need to get back to work. I'm not interested in starting anything with you, ok? Is that clear?"

I'm congratulating myself on my assertiveness, when he says, "Look at me. Do I look like a nut? A rapist? I just wanted a chance to meet you is all. I didn't know how else to do it. I guess I blew it. I'm sorry."

He looks like a whipped puppy and all of a sudden I'm feeling sorry for him and saying, "OK, look, I'm sorry, too. Meet me in the lobby after work and we'll have a cup of coffee and find out about each other." I must be crazy.

"Great! Great!"

He shakes my hand, smiles.

I have to admit it's a nice smile.

"I'll be there. My name is Charles Hastings, by the way. I'm the CEO and resident genius of Computron in your building. Smile, Laura, that genius part was a joke."

Laura!!!

"How do you know my name?"

"Don't look so worried," he says. "I heard your friend, the skinny one with the dark hair and purple eye shadow call you that in the lobby. Listen, just to prove I'm legitimate, I'll bring a colleague with me and he'll introduce us properly and verify what I've told you. And by the way... I saw you looking at my clothes. We're having a promotion party at the office this afternoon, see. Western theme. You know, we can round up customers for you. So..." He laughs. "I know I don't look like a CEO and the truth is, we're only a small company right now, but... I think I'm talking too much. I'm still nervous, but I have to tell you, Laura, you've made my day!"

He shakes my hand again and leaves. He really has a charming voice and he's not dumb after all. And maybe, just maybe, he might turn out to be Mr. Right. I find myself smiling as I head back to work. Mrs. Charles Hastings, I say to myself and laugh. It has a lovely ring.

PUZZLE

In my wildest dreams I never imagined that a jig-saw puzzle could land a person in a mental institution. I mean, it's not as though I said I saw aliens from outer space, or I killed somebody.

I've explained it over and over to the doctors, but do you think any of them really listened? Hell, I even showed it to them. But they pretended they didn't see it.

See, I was just working on a jigsaw puzzle one night, plain every day toy store puzzle, or at least that's what I thought, when all of a sudden I started wondering, I mean the idea just popped into my head, wouldn't it be funny if you could take a human body apart like that? Like, if you could take off a hand, say or an arm. Just sort of pull it off, no blood or anything, and then just put it back on if you wanted to.

I didn't plan it or anything. I guess I just sort of tugged at my wrist when I was thinking about it, not hard or anything, and I know you're going to think that this is peculiar I did myself, and I know the doctors do, but the hand and the wrist came right off, nice and neat like a piece of a puzzle.

Still, it scared me a little, so I tried sticking it back on. Sure enough it fitted right back in place. I thought maybe I was dreaming or something, so I pulled on the other arm, just a bit, and it came off, too, just as easy as the first one.

I put the arm back and yanked a bit on each of my legs and then my nose. It was the same with all of them, just about the best jig saw puzzle you can imagine.

After a bit, I got to wondering if it had anything to do with the puzzle I'd been working on or if it would work with other people, too. My little brother, Timmy, (he's five and a half and I'm fifteen) was in the room watching television. I went over and sort of pulled his wrist very gently.

He started screaming that I was hurting him and the arm didn't come off. My mom came into the room and she was yelling and pulling at me and the arm came off again, but she kept pretending she didn't notice it and kept yelling at me to leave Timmy alone.

"I wasn't trying to hurt him," I said "I just wanted to see if his arm would come off like mine did."

She started saying what was I talking about, and it was the dumbest excuse she ever heard. So I held out my detached arm to show her, but all she said was to stop talking crazy. You'd have thought, being my mom and all that she'd have been upset about it, but no, all she was, was mad at me for hurting Timmy, which I didn't, I mean I was real gentle.

So then I said, "Look mom, isn't it bitchin'. I can take my arm off and put it right back on, no blood or anything. And I can do it with my nose and legs, too.

The way she looked at me was real strange, so I said, "Let me show you." But when I did it with my leg she didn't seem impressed at all. She sort of backed away from me and said, "Is this some kind of joke? If it is, it isn't funny."

I didn't know if she meant was I pulling the leg off for a joke, or what. I didn't think it was funny either, just sort of amazing. So I said, "It didn't work with Timmy. Can I try it with you?" I walked over and pulled her arm, not hard, just to see if it would come off and she started yelling that I was hurting her.

Well, anyway, the next day she had me at the doctor's office. I don't know why. My arm didn't hurt or anything from taking it off or on. He talked to me for a little bit and I could tell he was sort of humoring me, as if I was crazy or something, so I said, "Look, I'll show you."

I took off my arm again and put it back on, but he didn't seem any more impressed than my mom had been. He gave my mom the name of this Dr. Gray. I think he's a psychiatrist, but to tell you the truth, I think he's the one who needs a psychiatrist, because there was the arm in plain sight and he pretended he didn't see it, just like my mother.

So that's when I realized that there was a plot going on. Just because they were jealous that I could do such fantastic things, they were making believe that they couldn't see something that was right in front of them. I decided to show the psychiatrist to see if he was in on the plot, and I pulled on his arm, too.

The next thing I know, here I am in this ward with a bunch of loonies and my mom has been crying her head off, (hey, I wonder if it would work just by crying). Still I can tell they're all in on the plot to ignore what I can do.

Yesterday I asked the recreational therapist if I could have a jig saw puzzle to work on but she said she'd have to talk to the doctor and see. You see how crazy this place is? They have to talk to a doctor before they can give you a simple jigsaw puzzle. It's enough to blow your mind.

FEAR

The man is skeletal, and his six foot frame exaggerates the effect. He barely drags his feet, as he maneuvers along the dry river bed. Yet, he is alert, head cocked, listening intently.

A faint snapping sound commands his attention. He crouches, freezing. The hair on his arms and back of his neck stands erect. He becomes a giant listening machine, all of his being like a single gigantic ear.

It is still. With infinite patience, he uncurls from his position, and resumes his slow progress. Twig snapping, he tells himself. Nothing to fear. Have to keep moving. Have to find water.

But there's the sound again, faint, yet definite. His body becomes rigid. Only his eyes stare, searching out the hillocks, the few stark trees, and the grass, just beyond the riverbed. Nothing.

Sweat breaks out on his forehead, runs maddeningly into his eyes. He knows he mustn't wipe it away. Keep still, still, he tells himself. Don't attract attention. There were two sounds. Two. Something is out there. What? He waits in an agony of indecision. Wait? How long? For what?

Instinct urges him to run, to escape whatever is there, but he waits. Time stretches, contracts. He has no idea how long he has been in this position.

Now he rises slowly, turning his head, scanning the area. He sees nothing, and begins his slow plodding again.

Then his eyes catch a flash of striped color, as with one mighty leap, the tiger materializes from the grass. He feels its warmth, and its great weight. He flails his arms, trying to fend it off.

Once more he hears, for the last time, a snapping sound. His neck is broken. He falls to the ground, and shrieks helplessly, as the tiger begins his meal.

THE BENEDICTION

There is no charitable way to put it. My cousin Clara was a singularly homely child. She'd had the misfortune to inherit the worst features from both sides of her family: her father's Dumbo ears and bulging eyes, her mother's receding chin and buck teeth.

If my Aunt Hannah had hoped that time would improve her daughter's situation, that as her skull grew, Clara's unfortunate physiognomy would become more proportionate, she must have been sorely disappointed as Clara reached adolescence. Even my cousin's one happy inheritance, an abundance of wavy dark hair, failed to conceal those ears, which stood almost at right angles to her face. Her eyes remained popped. Her chin withdrew further. Her overbite was as prominent as before.

I'm not sure plastic surgery had even been highly developed then, but in any case, this was in the middle of the depression. No one even considered it.

To compound the situation, Clara had been teased about her looks all through grade school. Her response was to develop a sharp tongue. She was a bright girl and perhaps her acerbic wit protected her, but at the same time, it increased her unpopularity. This state of affairs fed upon itself. Clara developed a personality that was at once negative, defensive and combative.

There was a final blow. In the Brooklyn ghettos, populated by immigrants from eastern and southern Europe and their offspring, even the first generation Americans, including the men, tended to be short, or of medium height at best. But Clara grew tall, five feet nine or ten, and large-boned. No one thought of it as a gift: it was regarded as another of Clara's misfortunes. Her defense was to cross her arms over her chest and hunch her back. The stance became permanent. The effect was disastrous.

When my sister, Lisa, delicate featured and petite, and Clara's junior by one year, began to date, Aunt Hannah and my mother (at Hannah's urging), prevailed upon Lisa to arrange a blind date for Clara. It was a disaster! Clara sized up the boy's five foot six and announced, "You won't want to go out with me. I'm too tall for you."

Surprise mingled with relief on the erstwhile date's face. You could tell he was glad to get out of it.

Lisa tried twice more. Each time was a catastrophe. Finally she put her foot down. She would have nothing more to do with it. Oddly enough, Clara seemed relieved.

When she was eighteen, my sister announced that she was getting married. Immediately a family feud broke out. They had brought to the New World an Old World custom. A younger sibling could not marry until an older sibling had done so. In our close-knit family, though this was not really the custom, the taboo extended to first cousins. Clara's mother was apoplectic: Lisa should wait until Clara married.

Lisa, however, flatly refused. She was not going to wait forever, she spat at my mother, and Clara was never going to get married. Never! My mother could see the logic of it. Aunt Hannah would not accept it. They shouted at each other. They stopped speaking. And Lisa got married.

It was a modest wedding, but Lisa was all in white, and her husband, Arnold, wore a tux, and the other aunts had prevailed upon both Clara and Aunt

Hannah to come to the wedding in the name of family peace. When the ceremony was over, the aunts celebrated another age-old custom. They surrounded Clara and chorused a benediction. It was spoken in a mixture of Hebrew and Yiddish. *"Mir tzuvba-deer hashem"*, they intoned (God willing, may you be the next bride).

I was three years younger than my sister, but at twenty, I, too, decided to get married. Again the feud broke out, and again the aunts persuaded Aunt Hannah and Clara to come to the ceremony. At its end, once more that chorus of well wishers surrounded Clara. *""Mir tzuvba-deer hashem""*, they said, and they meant it.

Soon it was Clara's younger brother's turn. Though Lisa and I had broken the ice for him, this was a more serious challenge. This was, after all, a sibling. But Joseph refused to wait. His bride, too, suggested, sotto voice, that waiting for Clara was waiting in vain. Aunt Hannah was beside herself, but what could she do? At the wedding, Hannah's sisters surrounded Clara again with their benediction.

Time passed and younger cousins, and then the next generation began to marry, and each wedding produced the same chorus of well-meaning harpies. If there was an element of oneupmanship in it over their own children's success, there was also a sincere wish that their niece would find happiness.

Clara adjusted to her single status. She had a good job and a close woman friend who was also single. They went out to movies and restaurants, and often spent evenings together watching television. Then, suddenly, without warning, Clara's friend married a fifty-five year old widower with three children. Clara reacted like a jilted lover. She was bereft, stricken, and furious. She regarded her friend's marriage as a defection and a betrayal. And she was terribly lonely.

Recently, Lisa's first grandchild married. Clara came to the wedding, but death had noticeably thinned the chorus which had always recited the benediction to her. Soon enough, the last of those old aunts will be gone as well, and I can't help wondering if, when that happens, when no echoes of "*Mir tzuvbadeer hashem.*" remain, Clara will be mightily relieved, or will the absence of the ancient blessing mean to her that all hope for marriage is gone forever.

LIGHTNING

All around me, on the 747 from Denver to Los Angeles, the passengers are restive. We have taken off, this afternoon, in a downpour, after a two-hour delay on the ground, caused by a fire which knocked out power to the control tower. At that, we have been luckier than some, who spent those two hours circling the airport.

Before we take off, the pilot announces over the intercom that the storm is local, and not to worry, we will be out of it in minutes. But as we climb higher, the clouds are enormous, dark and threatening.

We have barely reached cruising altitude, when we begin to see lightning within those clouds. Not once, but again and again, the lightning flashes all around our plane.

Again we hear the pilot's soothing drawl: "Don't be upset folks, we're equipped to fend off any strikes. Just sit back and relax."

The plane is shaking in the turbulence, and yet the flight attendants are going up the aisle with bottles of champagne and glasses, compliments of the airline. They have to hold on to the seat backs, or they'll be sprawled on the floor. I can only assume that the airline is bent on getting us all smashed, so we won't be scared.

When the nearest flight attendant is halfway up the aisle, the plane takes a sharp dip, and the proffered liquid spills all over a hapless passenger. The flight attendant apologizes and starts mopping him up, when the announcement comes over the intercom: "We are experiencing a little turbulence, folks. I suggest that all flight personnel take their seats for the next few minutes."

Easier said than done. The plane is riding the storm like a bucking bronco. The flight attendants can barely struggle to their seats.

The woman in front of me is praying. I can hear the "Hail Marys" clearly. Farther down the aisle, I can see the hands of a nun moving as she recites her rosary.

The "few minutes" stretches out to fifteen. Not only is the lightning flashing around us, but we are over the highest peaks of the Rockies, and they don't seem that far below us. I'm thinking, what if the plane drops like that again. Would we hit a mountain? I'm not ready to die. There are too many good things going on in my life.

I'm not the only one who's scared. Except for a screaming baby, there's a noticeable silence in the plane. Even the fake affability of the pilot is not coming over the airwaves. Obviously he has his hands full.

From the window, I can see blue skies up ahead, but we are still riding the storm. And then, the unthinkable happens. Lightning strikes the plane! No question about it. We feel the whole aircraft shudder. It's as if a giant hand was shaking the plane. Yet, somehow the 747 continues on its way, apparently unscathed.

Within another few minutes, we clear the last mountain range, and suddenly we are out in bright sunshine and azure skies.

Voices begin chattering again. The entire planeload seems to have held its collective breath, and now can return to normal.

The flight attendant comes back up the aisle and hands the hapless passenger who received the unwelcome christening, some sort of paper. Idly I wonder if it's a free flight or just an agreement to cover the cleaning bill.

Then she proceeds up the aisle again, pouring champagne, presumably so the rest of us won't feel cheated, or maybe just to calm us down.

The pilot's easy drawl comes on again. He makes no mention of the lightning strike. Does he really think we weren't aware of it?

"Well folks, that's it. It should be clear sailing now, all the way into LA."

PELICAN GRIEF

It's my brother-in-law, Jackson's, first outing since he suffered a stroke six months ago. He's still in a wheelchair, but so exhilarated to be able to start enjoying life again, that his mood is catching, and we're all upbeat.

My husband Roger and I had been visiting at my sister Jane's house in the fall, when Jackson had the stroke, and, of course, we'd stayed on until he had been sent to a rehab hospital.

This is the first time we've seen him since then, and we're shocked at his appearance. Jackson had always been a jock, trim and athletic and deeply tanned. Now he's a pasty white and somewhat shrunken. He looks ten years older than Roger, though they're both fifty-three.

The contrast is all the more marked, because Roger is six feet four, and built like the redwood trees back home near Yosemite where we live. He lifts weights, and could play Sampson in one of those B movies if he had a little more hair.

For this first outing we've decided to go to Tarpon Springs, not far from Jane and Jackson's home on the west coast of Florida, because it's the nearest town of any interest. For now, Tampa is too far away.

What's interesting about Tarpon Springs is that it is, or was, a sponge diver's town, settled by Greeks, who transported their skills from their native islands. We browse through a small privately owned museum looking at an exhibit describing the techniques and equipment used to gather and dry sponges. Next, we stop at a number of stalls that sell beach-type knick-knacks, and of course all types and grades of sponges.

But now we're hungry, and we wander in for lunch at a small family-run Greek restaurant. The shish kebabs and dolmas are wonderful, and we celebrate with the best baklava pastries I've ever had. They're packed with walnuts and raisins, and almost dripping honey, and the fila pastry is flaky and tender. By the time we finish, we're all in a wonderful mood. If Jackson's strength holds out, we'll wander along the waterfront, visit one or two tourist shops, and then head back home.

Roger pushes Jackson's wheelchair along the walkway fronting the water so he can watch the ungainly pelicans hovering over the small bay. The birds wheel and flap their wings awkwardly, lifting their heavy bodies a few feet into the air, and then suddenly diving into the water to snatch a fish.

One of the pelicans is perched on a piling at the end of a short pier, and to give Jackson a better look at it, Roger takes the wheelchair out onto the pier, and Jane and I follow. Perhaps there's a nest out there, because as we watch, one of the pelicans dives straight down toward my husband.

Roger is so startled that he lets go of the wheelchair. It's brake isn't on and the chair, with Jackson strapped into it, goes sailing off the pier, and into the water.

Instantly, Roger dives in after it, shoes and all, and manages to grab the back of the wheelchair just as it's going under. It's terribly heavy, and Roger yells for us to unstrap the seat belt and pull Jackson out.

My sister and I doff our pumps, but otherwise fully clothed, dive into the water too, and as I help Roger hold the chair, Jane releases the seatbelt and extracts Jackson.

The wheelchair is too heavy for us and it's about to sink, when a bystander tosses Roger one end of a rope that someone has brought, and Roger ties it to the chair.

As Jane and I swim and pull Jackson the few feet to shore, the people holding the rope guide the wheelchair in, though it takes about six of them to keep it from sinking, even with Roger holding it up from the rear.

Finally we're all back on the walkway, sopping wet, especially Roger, whose shoes are sloshing water. Someone from a local restaurant brings us towels, and we dry ourselves off as best we can. We buy a large beach towel from a tourist shop, and wrap it around Jackson. Wiping off the wheelchair, we settle him into it, and return to the car from our outing, bedraggled and miserable, threatening to shoot the next pelican that dares to cross our path.

Made in the USA
San Bernardino, CA
22 May 2018